16

17

18

19

20

21

22

23

24

25

26

27

28

29

30

Once Upon a Time . . .

there lived a very selfish and spoiled young Prince.

One cold winter's night, an old beggar woman came to his castle and offered him a single red rose in return for shelter.

Repulsed by her ugliness, the Prince heartlessly turned her away. The old woman warned him not to be deceived by appearances, for true beauty is found only within. But, again, he dismissed her.

Suddenly, the old woman turned into a beautiful Enchantress, who cast a spell on the castle and transformed the Prince into a hideous Beast. The Enchantress left the Beast with a magic mirror and the rose. If he could learn to love someone and earn her love in return before the last rose petal fell, the spell would be broken. If not, he would remain a Beast forever.

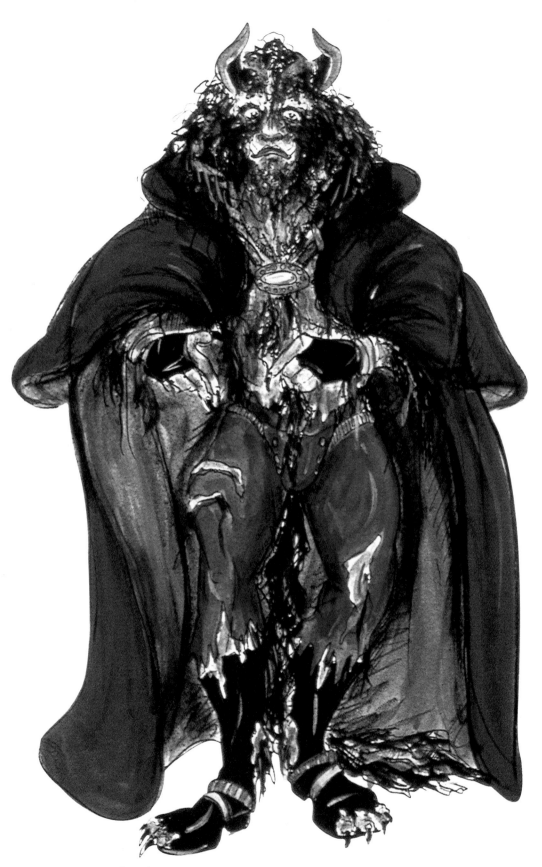

As the years passed, the Beast lost all hope. For
who could ever learn to love a Beast?

Disney's Beauty and the Beast

A CELEBRATION OF THE BROADWAY MUSICAL

BY DONALD FRANTZ WITH SUE HEINEMANN
FOREWORD BY ALAN MENKEN

BASED ON WALT DISNEY PRODUCTIONS' PRESENTATION OF
"BEAUTY AND THE BEAST"

MUSIC BY
ALAN MENKEN

LYRICS BY
HOWARD ASHMAN & TIM RICE

BOOK BY
LINDA WOOLVERTON

SCENIC DESIGN
STAN MEYER

LIGHTING DESIGN
NATASHA KATZ

COSTUME DESIGN
ANN HOULD-WARD

HAIR DESIGN
DAVID H. LAWRENCE

ILLUSIONS
JIM STEINMEYER & JOHN GAUGHAN

PROSTHETICS
JOHN DODS

PRODUCTION SUPERVISOR
JEREMIAH J. HARRIS

GENERAL MANAGEMENT
DODGER PRODUCTIONS

PRODUCTION STAGE MANAGER
JAMES HARKER

PRESS REPRESENTATIVE
BONEAU/BRYAN-BROWN

DANCE ARRANGEMENTS
GLEN KELLY

MUSICAL COORDINATOR
JOHN MILLER

CASTING
JAY BINDER

FIGHT DIRECTOR
RICK SORDELET

MUSICAL SUPERVISION &
VOCAL ARRANGEMENTS
DAVID FRIEDMAN

MUSIC DIRECTION &
INCIDENTAL MUSIC ARRANGEMENTS
MICHAEL KOSARIN

ORCHESTRATIONS
DANNY TROOB

CHOREOGRAPHY BY
MATT WEST

DIRECTED BY
ROBERT JESS ROTH

A ROUNDTABLE PRESS BOOK

HYPERION

NEW YORK

"Belle"
"Belle (Reprise)"
"Gaston"
"Gaston (Reprise)"
"Be Our Guest"
"Something There"
"Human Again"
"Beauty and the Beast"
"The Mob Song"
"Beauty and the Beast (Reprise)"
Lyrics by Howard Ashman, Music by Alan Menken
© 1991 Walt Disney Music Company and Wonderland Music Company, Inc.
All Rights Reserved. Used by Permission

"No Matter What"
"No Matter What (Reprise)"
"Home"
"Home (Reprise)"
"How Long Must This Go On?"
"If I Can't Love Her"
"If I Can't Love Her (Reprise)"
"Maison des Lunes"
"Transformation"
Music by Alan Menken, Lyrics by Tim Rice
© 1994 Wonderland Music Company, Inc., Menken Music, Trunksong Music Ltd. and Walt Disney Music Company.
All Rights Reserved. Used by Permission.

Special Thanks to:
WALT DISNEY PICTURES FEATURE ANIMATION DIVISION
for the creation of the Academy Award-winning film
Beauty and the Beast, upon which the stage version is based:
DON HAHN, PRODUCER;
GARY TROUSDALE, DIRECTOR;
KIRK WISE, DIRECTOR;
and to the many talented artists and animators who contributed to the film;

also to:
TOM CHILD, INITIAL CONCEPTUAL DEVELOPMENT;

and:
FRANK WELLS,
JEFFREY KATZENBERG,
RON LOGAN,
for their help with the original Broadway production of
Beauty and the Beast

FOR WALT DISNEY THEATRICAL PRODUCTIONS
Producer: Robert W. McTyre
Associate Producer: Donald Frantz
Production Manager: Bettina Buckley
Casting Director: Ron Rodriguez
Pyrotechnic Design: Tylor Wymer
Audio Design: Bill Platt

FOR ROUNDTABLE PRESS
Directors: Susan E. Meyer, Marsha Melnick
Executive Editor: Amy T. Jonak
Assistant Editor: Megan Keiler
Design: Nai Chang
Production: Bill Rose
Production Assistant: Steven Rosen

FOR HYPERION
Editor: Wendy Lefkon
Editorial Assistant: Monique Peterson

ADDITIONAL CREDITS
Press Liaisons: Chris Boneau, Patty Onagan, and Miguel Tuason, Boneau/Bryan-Brown; Rick Miramontez and Ron Hofmann, Rick Miramontez Company
Production Photography: Joan Marcus, Marc Bryan-Brown
Other Photographs by Joan Marcus: pages 12, 97, 98, 152
Costume Art: Ann Hould-Ward
Costume Photography: Tim Blacker, Tracy Christensen, and David Paulin
Set Art: Brigette Altenhaus, David Blankenship, Mark Fitzgibbons, Sarah Lambert, Edmund A. LeFevre, Jr., Stan Meyer, Michael Todd Potter, Scott Shaffer, Bill Sturrock, and Brian Webb
Prosthetics Photography: John Dods Studio
Hair Work Photography: David H. Lawrence
Quotations from Susan Egan from KCAL Channel 9 News (April 12, 1995) and article by Christopher Trela in Orange County *Metro* (April 15, 1995)
Quotations from Terrence Mann from article by Lynette Rice in Los Angeles *Daily News* (April 11, 1995), KNBC Channel 4 News (April 10, 1995), KTTV Channel 11 News (April 12, 1995), and KCAL Channel 9 News (April 10, 1995)

Library of Congress Cataloging-in-Publication Data
Frantz, Donald.
    Beauty and the Beast : a celebration of the Broadway musical / Donald Frantz with Sue Heinemann : foreword by Alan Menken ; complete lyrics by Howard Ashman and Tim Rice ; script excerpts by Linda Wolverton.
      p. cm.
    Includes libretto.
    ISBN 0-7868-6179-7
  1. Menken, Alan. Beauty and the beast. 2. Musicals—Production and direction. 3. Musicals—Stage guides. 4. Musicals—Librettos.
I. Heinemann, Sue, 1948– . II. Ashman, Howard. III. Rice, Tim.
IV. Wolverton, Linda. V. Menken, Alan. Beauty and the beast.
Libretto. VI. Title.
ML410.M F
782.1'4—dc20
                            95-32295
                              CIP
                              MN

First Edition
10 9 8 7 6 5 4 3 2 1

Contents

Foreword

Alan Menken

There is no more satisfying experience than working on a Broadway show, especially a *hit* Broadway show! Growing up, I was surrounded by a family that loved Broadway musicals. Regularly, we gathered around my father at the piano, and as he played and we sang, the house filled with the sounds of Rodgers and Hart, the Gershwins, Rodgers and Hammerstein, Frank Loesser, Lerner and Loewe, and all the other great Broadway songwriters.

As a child, I was introduced to the power of the American musical through shows like *My Fair Lady, Fiorello,* and *The Sound of Music.* So, it is an awesome experience for me to witness today's generation of children having a similar experience seeing *Beauty and the Beast.* There is no form like the musical. It gets inside of us, haunts us, and somehow changes us for the better.

Admittedly, when I was first informed that Disney had chosen *Beauty* as its first Broadway production, I had my doubts. Disney had never produced a large-scale musical, much less adapted an animated film onto the Broadway stage. In my mind I pictured a theme-park spectacle with huge foam-headed characters racing around to canned music.

But any fears I had were allayed several months later, when I was invited to Los Angeles for a presentation given by the director, Rob Roth, and the creative team he had assembled around him. They showed us set and costume designs, as well as the structural changes they envisioned. Their seriousness impressed me. Not only were they genuine fans of the animated feature, but they were also an incredibly enthusiastic group of talented people, who were truly devoted to live, legitimate theater. The excitement of their creative process was contagious, and that excitement continued throughout the development of the Broadway show. Also, Michael Eisner and Jeffrey Katzenberg proved to be ideal producers—extremely generous, but tough when they needed to be. It was a fantastic experience from start to finish.

An especially rewarding aspect of bringing *Beauty and the Beast* to Broadway was the chance to introduce a "new" song Howard and I had written for the project. Years after Howard's death, "Human Again" was reborn in the stage production.

Howard was a remarkable talent, a wonderful director, scriptwriter, and lyricist. His input was critical to the initial creation of *Beauty;* he figured out how to enliven the story and strengthen the central characters by inventing the "objects," who are servants who have fallen under the same spell as the Beast. Howard didn't live to see the finished film; he died in March 1991, six months before the film's release. He never knew how people would love the film, let alone how people would set box-office records rushing to see the Broadway show.

In all of our work, for both stage and film, Howard and I were a part of the Broadway musical tradition. Our songs strive to tell the story and elevate its emotional content. Music is essential to the experience of the story—an aspect that is impossible to convey in a book. In the best musicals, you should be able to gain a sense of the story just by listening to the musical score, without any words.

With that in mind, Howard and I always chose song moments where the musical style could be very specific, allowing you to make an association while taking you to another place. *Beauty and the Beast* is full of moments like that.

In the "Prologue," for example, the music is deliberately impressionistic, suggesting "long ago and far away," in the mythical world of a fairy tale. Then the music shifts to suggesting an idyllic pastorale as Belle walks to town singing, "Little town, it's a quiet village. . . ." When she reaches the town, to the sound of the villagers' greeting— "Bonjour! Bonjour! Bonjour!"—the music bursts into a classical style . . . a little Mozart operetta. With "Belle," the "pact" with the audience is sealed. This is a magical fairy tale, in which the characters will sing their deepest thoughts and feelings. It will be romantic and comedic.

Beauty and the Beast is drawn in primary colors, with many stark contrasts. When the music is idyllic, it's storybook idyllic, and when it's dark, it's ominously, relentlessly, melodramatically dark. The up-beat production fireworks of "Be Our Guest" are set back to back with the Beast's soul-searching lament, "If I Can't Love Her."

As the Act One curtain falls, if we've done our job correctly, the audience is left with a cliff-hanger. It all seems hopeless, for the Beast has driven Belle away, and yet there is still a glimmer of hope. The music promises that anything can happen. Musicals are about characters who go bravely forward in the face of adversity. They are about overcoming immense obstacles to realize great dreams.

Although I could separately describe each song in *Beauty,* the impact of a show comes from the unique blend of styles and colors that make up a score. I hope that in reading the lyrics reprinted in this book, many of you will already be familiar with the music, so you can "hear" the songs. And for those who have not yet experienced the stage production of *Beauty and the Beast,* I hope that the images and words in this book will invite you to enjoy for yourself the wonders of live theater.

ALAN MENKEN

NEW YORK, 1995

PART ONE

The Story

Belle . . .

In a small, provincial town, a beautiful and intelligent young woman named Belle yearns for adventure.

BELLE: *Little town, it's a quiet village.*
Ev'ry day like the one before.
Little town, full of little people
Waking up to say . . .

TOWNSFOLK: *Bonjour!*
Bonjour!
Bonjour! Bonjour! Bonjour!

BELLE: *There goes the baker with his tray, like always,*
The same old bread and rolls to sell.
Ev'ry morning just the same
Since the morning that we came
To this poor provincial town.

BAKER (speaking): Good morning, Belle!
BELLE: Morning, Monsieur!
BAKER: Where are you off to?
BELLE: The bookshop. I just finished the most wonderful story about a beanstalk and an ogre and a . . .
BAKER: That's nice. Marie! The baguettes! Hurry up!

TOWNSFOLK: *Look, there she goes. That girl is strange, no question.*
Dazed and distracted, can't you tell?
Never part of any crowd,
'Cause her head's up on some cloud.
No denying she's a funny girl, that Belle.

MAN 1: *Bonjour.*
WOMAN 1: *Good day.*
MAN 1: *How is your fam'ly?*
WOMAN 2: *Bonjour.*
MAN 2: *Good day.*
WOMAN 2: *How is your wife?*
WOMAN 3: *I need six eggs.*
WOMAN 4: *That's too expensive!*
BELLE: *There must be more than this provincial life!*

(Belle talks with Bookseller, who gives her a book.)

SUSAN EGAN, GORDON STANLEY

18

TOWNSFOLK: *Look, there she goes. That girl is so peculiar.*
    I wonder if she's feeling well.
    With a dreamy, far-off look
    And her nose stuck in a book,
    What a puzzle to the rest of us is Belle!

BELLE: *Oh . . . isn't this amazing?*
    It's my fav'rite part because . . . you'll see.
    Here's where she meets Prince Charming,
    But she won't discover that it's him
    'Til Chapter Three.

WOMAN: *Now, it's no wonder that her name means "Beauty."*
    Her looks have got no parallel.
MAN 1: *But behind that fair facade,*
    I'm afraid she's rather odd.
MAN 2: *Very diff'rent from the rest of us.*
TOWNSFOLK: *She's nothing like the rest of us.*
    Yes, diff'rent from the rest of us is Belle.

(Gaston and Lefou enter)
GASTON: *Right from the moment when I met her, saw her,*
    I said, "She's gorgeous," and I fell.
    Here in town there's only she

Who is beautiful as me.
So I'm making plans to woo and marry Belle.

SILLY GIRLS: *Look there he goes!*
Isn't he dreamy?
Monsieur Gaston!
Oh, he's so cute!
Be still, my heart!
I'm hardly breathing!
He's such a tall, dark, strong and handsome brute!

WOMAN 1: *Bonjour!*
GASTON: *Pardon.*
BELLE: *Good day.*
WOMAN 2: *Mais oui.*
WOMAN 3: *You call this bacon?*
WOMAN 4: *What lovely grapes!*
MAN 1: *Some cheese.*
WOMAN 5: *Ten yards.*
MAN 2: *One pound.*
GASTON: *'Scuse me!*
MAN 3: *I'll get the knife.*
GASTON: *Please let me through!*
WOMAN 6: *This bread . . .*
WOMAN 7: *These fish . . .*
WOMAN 6: *It's stale.*
WOMAN 7: *They smell!*
MEN: *Madame's mistaken.*
WOMEN: *Well, maybe so.*
TOWNSFOLK: *Good morning! Oh, good morning!*
BELLE: *There must be more than this provincial life.*
GASTON: *Just watch, I'm going to make Belle my wife!*

TOWNSFOLK: *Look, there she goes. A girl who's strange but special.*
A most peculiar mad'moiselle.
WOMEN: *It's a pity and a sin.*
MEN: *She doesn't quite fit in.*
TOWNSFOLK: *'Cause she really is a funny girl.*
A beauty, but a funny girl.
She really is a funny girl . . . that Belle!

After brushing off Gaston's attentions, Belle hurries home
to help her father, Maurice, with his latest invention. She
asks him if he, like the townsfolk, thinks she's odd.

No Matter What . . .

MAURICE: *No, I'm not odd, nor you.*
   No fam'ly ever saner,
   Except one uncle who . . . well, maybe let that pass.
   In all you say or do,
   You couldn't make it plainer.
   You are your mother's daughter; therefore you are class.

BELLE: *So I should just accept*
   I'm simply not like them?

MAURICE: *They are the common herd.*
   And you can take my word:
   You are unique: crème de la crème.

No matter what you do,
I'm on your side.
And if my point of view
Is somewhat misty-eyed,
There's nothing clearer in my life
Than what I wish and feel for you,
And that's a lot . . .
No matter what.

BELLE: *No matter what they say,*
You make me proud.
I love the funny way
You stand out from the crowd.

MAURICE: *It's my intention my invention shows the world out there one day*
Just what we've got . . .
BOTH: *No matter what.*

MAURICE: *Now, some may say all fathers just exaggerate.*
BELLE: *That ev'ry daughter's great?*
MAURICE: *You are!*
BELLE: *And ev'ry daughter tends to say her father's tops.*
MAURICE: *She pulls out all the stops*
To praise him.
BOTH: *And quite rightly!*

MAURICE: *No matter what the pain,*
We've come this far.
I pray that you remain
Exactly as you are.
This really is a case of father knowing best.
BELLE: *And daughter too!*

MAURICE: *You're never strange.*
BELLE: *Don't ever change.*
BOTH: *You're all I've got,*
No matter what.

SUSAN EGAN, TOM BOSLEY

Maurice tries out his invention . . . and it works. Delighted,
he rides off through the woods to the fair on his contraption.

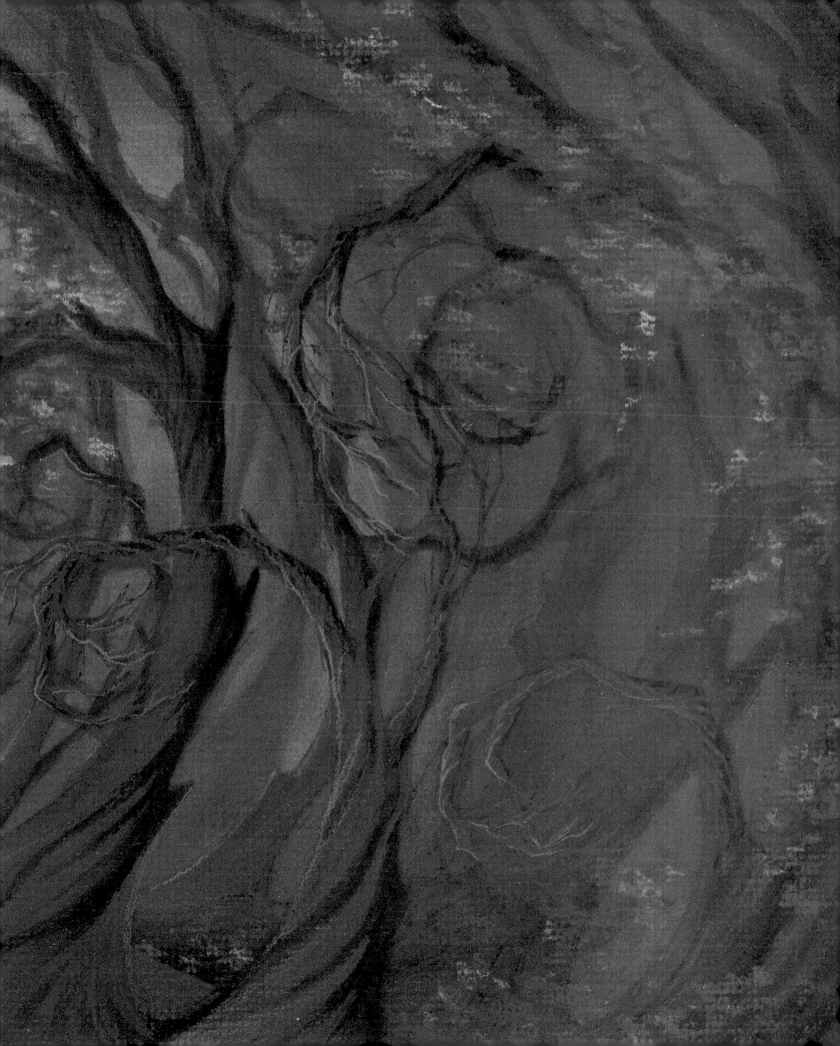

No Matter What . . .

REPRISE

MAURICE: *First prize is nearly mine.*
　　　It's quite my best invention.
　　　So simple, yet complex. So massive, yet so small.

　　　This triumph of design
　　　Will be my old-age pension.
　　　That is, provided I can find the fair at all.

　　　I must have missed a sign . . .
　　　I should have paid attention . . .
　　　(Wolf howls)
　　　That's not a nightingale, and not a mating call.

Fleeing from the wolves, Maurice bangs desperately on the castle door, which opens onto a huge, eerie space. There Maurice is soon made comfortable by a talking candelabra (Lumiere), mantle clock (Cogsworth), and feather-duster (Babette)—until the furious Beast grabs him. Meanwhile, Gaston pursues Belle.

28

Me . . .

GASTON: *You've been dreaming*
  Just one dream
  Nearly all your life.
  Hoping, scheming
  Just one theme:
  Will you be a wife?
  Will you be some he-man's property?
  Good news! That he-man's me!

  This equation,
  Girl plus man,
  Doesn't help just you.
  On occasion
  Women can
  Have their uses too.
  Mainly to extend the fam'ly tree.
  Pumpkin, extend with me!

GASTON: *We'll be raising sons galore,*
BELLE: *Inconceivable!*
GASTON: *Each built six foot four!*
BELLE: *Unbelievable!*
GASTON: *Each one stuffed with ev'ry Gaston gene!*
BELLE: *I'm not hearing this!*
GASTON: *You'll be keeping house with pride.*
BELLE: *Just incredible!*
GASTON: *Oh so gratified*
BELLE: *So unweddable!*
GASTON: *That you are part of this idyllic scene.*

GASTON (speaking): Picture this: A rustic hunting
  lodge, my latest kill roasting over the fire, my little
  wife massaging my feet, while the little ones play
  on the floor with the dogs. We'll have six or seven!
BELLE: Dogs?
GASTON: No, Belle! Strapping boys . . . like me!
BELLE: Imagine that!

GASTON: *I can see that we will share*
  All that love implies.
  We shall be the perfect pair;

Rather like my thighs.
You are face to face with destiny!
All roads lead to . . .
The best things in life are . . .
All's well that ends with me!

Escape me?
There's no way.
Certain as "Do, Re,"
Belle, when you marry . . .
Me!

Before Gaston can take another breath, Belle
fends him off, ducking into her cottage. Later,
she sings of her relief.

Belle . . .
REPRISE

BELLE: *"Madame Gaston!" Can't you just see it?*
"Madame Gaston" his "little wife."
No sir. Not me! I guarantee it.
I want much more than this provincial life.

I want adventure in the great wide somewhere!
I want it more than I can tell!
And for once it might be grand
To have someone understand.
I want so much more than they've got planned.

Lefou runs in, wearing Maurice's scarf, and Belle realizes
something is wrong. She rushes off to find Maurice, only
to discover him imprisoned in the castle. Belle begs the
Beast to release her father, but the Beast refuses. In desperation Belle offers to take her father's place, and immediately
the Beast orders a gargoyle to drag Maurice off. "Papa!"
Belle cries out, but he is gone before she has a chance to
say good-bye. Belle is left alone with the Beast, who gruffly
escorts her to her room.

Home . . .

BELLE: *Yes, I made the choice*
For papa, I will stay.
But I don't deserve to lose my freedom in this way,
You monster!
If you think that what you've done is right, well then,
You're a fool!
Think again!

Is this home?
Is this where I should learn to be happy?
Never dreamed
That a home could be dark and cold.
I was told
Ev'ry day in my childhood:
Even when you grow old,
Home should be where the heart is.
Never were words so true!
My heart's far, far away.
Home is too.

What I'd give to return
To the life that I knew lately.
And to think I complained
Of that dull provincial town.

Is this home?
Am I here for a day or forever?
Shut away
From the world until who knows when.
Oh, but then,
As my life has been altered once,
It can change again.
Build higher walls around me
Change ev'ry lock and key.
Nothing lasts,
Nothing holds
All of me.
My heart's far, far away,
Home and free!

A teapot (Mrs. Potts) enters, offering a cup of tea. She and an armoire (Madame de la Grande Bouche) try to console Belle.

Home . . .
REPRISE

MRS. POTTS: *I hope that we'll be friends,*
Though I don't know you well.
If anyone can make the most of living here,
Then, Belle, it's you.
And who knows?
You may find
Home here, too!

In the tavern Gaston broods over Belle's rejection. His pals try to cheer him up.

Gaston . . .

LEFOU: *Gosh, it disturbs me to see you, Gaston,*
Looking so down in the dumps.
Ev'ry guy here'd love to be you, Gaston,
Even when taking your lumps.
There's no man in town as admired as you.
You're ev'ryone's favorite guy.
Ev'ryone's awed and inspired by you,
And it's not very hard to see why.

No one's slick as Gaston.
No one's quick as Gaston.
No one's neck's as incredibly thick as Gaston's.
For there's no man in town half as manly.

Perfect! A pure paragon!
You can ask any Tom, Dick or Stanley
And they'll tell you whose team
They prefer to play on.

CHORUS: *No one's been like Gaston,*
A kingpin like Gaston.
LEFOU: *No one's got a swell cleft in his chin like Gaston.*
GASTON: *As a specimen, yes, I'm intimidating!*
CHORUS: *My, what a guy, that Gaston!*
Give five "hurrahs"! Give twelve "hip-hips"!
LEFOU: *Gaston is the best and the rest is all drips.*

MEN: *No one fights like Gaston,*
   Douses lights like Gaston.
LEFOU: *In a wrestling match, nobody bites like Gaston.*
SILLY GIRLS: *For there's no one as burly and brawny.*
GASTON: *As you see, I've got biceps to spare.*
LEFOU: *Not a bit of him's scraggly or scrawny.*
GASTON: *That's right! And ev'ry last inch of me's covered with hair.*

CHORUS: *No one hits like Gaston.*
   Matches wits like Gaston.
LEFOU: *In a spitting match, nobody spits like Gaston.*
GASTON: *I'm especially good at expectorating. Ptooey!*
CHORUS: *Ten points for Gaston!*

GASTON: *When I was a lad I ate four dozen eggs*
   Ev'ry morning to help me get large.
   And now that I'm grown

I eat five dozen eggs
So I'm roughly the size of a barge!

CHORUS: *Oh, ahhh, wow!*
   My what a guy, that Gaston.

CHORUS: *No one shoots like Gaston,*
   Makes those beauts like Gaston.
LEFOU: *Then goes tromping around in his boots like Gaston.*
GASTON: *I use antlers in all of my decorating!*
CHORUS: *My what a guy,*
   Gaston.

Maurice races in, begging for help in saving Belle from the Beast. Laughing, Gaston's friends agree to help him out . . . out the door.

Gaston . . .

REPRISE

GASTON: *Lefou, I'm afraid I've been thinking.*

LEFOU: *A dangerous pastime.*

GASTON: *I know.*

> *But that wacky old coot*
> *Is Belle's father,*
> *And his sanity's only "so-so."*
> *Now the wheels in my head*
> *Have been turning*
> *Since I looked at that loony old man.*
> *See, I've promised myself*
> *I'd be married to Belle*
> *And right now I'm evolving a plan!*

> *If I . . .* (whispers)

LEFOU: Yes?

GASTON: *Then we . . .* (whispers)

LEFOU: *No! Would she . . .* (whispers)

GASTON: Guess!

LEFOU: Now I get it.

BOTH: Let's go!

BOTH: *No one plots like Gaston.*

GASTON: *Takes cheap shots like Gaston.*

LEFOU: *Plans to persecute harmless crackpots like Gaston.*

GASTON: *Yes, I'm endlessly, wildly resourceful.*

LEFOU: *As down to the depths you descend.*

GASTON: *I won't even be mildly remorseful,*

BOTH: *Just as long as I [you] get what I [you] want in the end!*

GASTON: *Who has brains like Gaston?*

LEFOU: *Entertains like Gaston?*

BOTH: *Who can make up these endless refrains like Gaston?*
> *And his marriage we soon will be celebrating.*
> *My, what a guy, Gaston!*

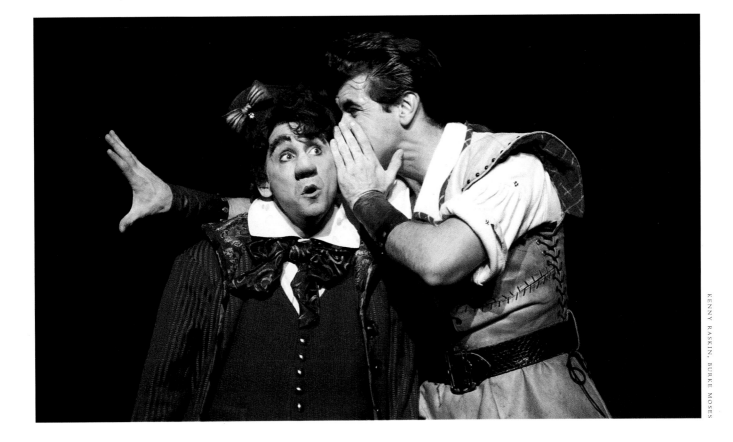

In the castle Lumiere and Mrs. Potts encourage the Beast to act like a gentleman around Belle. But when Cogsworth reports that Belle refuses to come to dinner, the Beast storms up to her room. Struggling with his temper, he tries to ask nicely, but Belle still refuses—and the Beast goes off in a rage. Gazing into his magic mirror, he watches as Belle tells Madame de la Grande Bouche she wants nothing to do with him.

How Long Must This Go On? . . .

BEAST: *How long must this go on,*
  This cruel trick of fate?
  I simply made one careless wrong decision.

  And then the witch was gone
  And left me in this state,
  An object of revulsion and derision.

  Hated . . .
  Is there no one
  Who can show me
  How to win the world's forgiveness?

Glancing at the rose, the Beast moans as another petal falls. At the other end of the castle, Belle realizes she's hungry and wanders off in search of food.

TERRENCE MANN

Be Our Guest...

LUMIERE: *Be our guest! Be our guest!*
> *Put our service to the test.*
> *Tie your napkin 'round your neck, chérie,*
> *And we'll provide the rest.*
> *Soup du jour!*
> *Hot hors d'oeuvres!*
> *Why, we only live to serve.*
> *Try the gray stuff.*

CHIP: *It's delicious!*

LUMIERE: *Don't believe me? Ask the dishes.*
> *They can sing! They can dance!*
> *After all, Miss, this is France!*
> *And a dinner here is never second best.*
> *Go on, unfold your menu.*
> *Take a glance and then you'll*
> *Be our guest.*
> *Oui, our guest.*
> *Be our guest!*

CHORUS: *Beef ragout!*
> *Cheese soufflé!*
> *Pie and pudding "en flambé"!*

LUMIERE: *We'll prepare and serve with flair*
> *A culinary cabaret.*
> *You're alone and you're scared,*
> *But the banquet's all prepared.*
> *No one's gloomy or complaining*
> *While the flatware's entertaining.*
> *We tell jokes! I do tricks*
> *With my fellow candlesticks.*

CHORUS: *And it's all in perfect taste, that you can bet!*
> *Come on and lift your glass.*
> *You've won your own free pass to*
> *Be our guest!*

LUMIERE: *If you're stressed*
> *It's fine dining we suggest.*

CHORUS: *Be our guest! Be our guest! Be our guest!*

Be our guest! Be our guest!
Get your worries off your chest.
Let us say for your entrée
We've an array; may we suggest:
Try the bread! Try the soup!
When the croutons loop de loop.
It's a treat for any diner.
Don't believe me? Ask the china.

Singing pork! Dancing veal!
What an entertaining meal!
How could anyone be gloomy or depressed?
We'll make you shout "encore"
And send us out for more.
So, be our guest!

LUMIERE: *Be our guest!*

CHORUS: *Be our guest!*

MRS. POTTS: *It's a guest! It's a guest!*
> *Sakes alive. Well, I'll be blessed.*
> *Wine's been poured and, thank the Lord,*
> *I've had the napkins freshly pressed.*
> *With dessert she'll want tea.*
> *And, my dear, that's fine with me.*
> *While the cups do their soft-shoeing,*
> *I'll be bubbling, I'll be brewing.*
> *I'll get warm, piping hot.*
> *Heaven's sakes, is that a spot?*
> *Clean it up! We want the company impressed!*

CHORUS: *We've got a lot to do!*

MRS. POTTS: *Is it one lump or two*
> *For you, our guest?*

CHORUS: *She's our guest!*

MRS. POTTS: *She's our guest!*

CHORUS: *She's our guest!*
> *Be our guest!*
> *Be our guest!*
> *Be our guest!*

LUMIERE: *Life is so unnerving*
  For a servant who's not serving.
  He's not whole without a soul to wait upon.
  Ah, those good old days when we were useful . . .
  Suddenly those good old days are gone.

  Ten years we've been rusting,
  Needing so much more than dusting.
  Needing exercise, a chance to use our skills!
  Most days, we just sit around the castle,
  Flabby, fat and lazy.
  You walked in and oops-a-daisy!

CHORUS: *Be our guest! Be our guest!*
  Our command is your request.
  It's been years since we've had anybody here,

And we're obsessed
With your meal, with your ease,
Yes, indeed, we aim to please.

While the candlelight's still glowing,
Let us help you. We'll keep going
Course by course, one by one,
'Til you shout: "Enough! I'm done!"
Then we'll sing you off to sleep as you digest.
Tonight you'll prop your feet up.
But for now, let's eat up.

Be our guest!
Be our guest!
Be our guest!
Please, be our guest!

TERRENCE MANN

While the Beast carefully carries a tray of food to Belle's room, Cogsworth and Lumiere take Belle on a tour of the castle. But Belle slips away to explore the mysterious, forbidden West Wing . . . and the Beast discovers her there, just about to touch the fragile rose. Furious, he snarls and grabs at her, frightening her so much that she flees from the castle.

If I Can't Love Her . . .

BEAST: *And in my twisted face*
There's not the slightest trace
Of anything that even hints of kindness.
And from my tortured shape,
No comfort, no escape.
I see, but deep within is utter blindness.

Hopeless,
As my dream dies.
As the time flies,
Love a lost illusion.
Helpless,
Unforgiven.
Cold and driven
To this sad conclusion.

No beauty could move me,
No goodness improve me.
No power on Earth, if I can't love her.
No passion could reach me,
No lesson could teach me
How I could have loved her and made her love me too.
If I can't love her, then who?

Long ago I should have seen
All the things I could have been.
Careless and unthinking, I moved onward.

No pain could be deeper,
No life could be cheaper.
No point anymore, if I can't love her.
No spirit could win me.
No hope left within me,
Hope I could have loved her and that she'd set me free.
But it's not to be.
If I can't love her,
Let the world be done with me.

(The curtain falls, ending Act One.)

As wolves snap at Belle, the Beast rushes in and flings them off. Poised to escape, Belle realizes the Beast is hurt and turns to help him. Back in the castle, she gently tends to his wounds . . . and he lets her. To warm them up, Mrs. Potts suggests some soup.

Something There . . .

BELLE: *There's something sweet*
   And almost kind,
   But he was mean and he was coarse and unrefined.
   But now he's dear and so unsure.
   I wonder why I didn't see it there before.

(Belle goes off to change her clothes.)

BEAST: *She glanced this way,*
   I thought I saw.
   And when we touched she didn't shudder at my paw.
   No, it can't be. I'll just ignore.
   But then, she never looked at me that way before.

SUSAN EGAN, TERRENCE MANN

(When Belle returns, the Beast shyly asks her to close her eyes and leads her to a surprise. On opening her eyes she gasps to see a library, filled with books. "It's yours!" the Beast says, as Belle delightedly explores the shelves.)

BELLE: *New, and a bit alarming.*
    Who'd have ever thought that this could be?
    True that he's no Prince Charming,
    But there's something in him
    That I simply didn't see.

(Belle begins to read the story of King Arthur to the Beast, who never learned to read.)

LUMIERE: *Well, who'd have thought?*
MRS. POTTS: *Well, bless my soul!*
COGSWORTH: *Well, who'd have known?*
MRS. POTTS: *Well, who indeed?*

LUMIERE: *And who'd have guessed they'd come*
  Together on their own?
MRS. POTTS: *It's so peculiar.*
ALL THREE: *Well, wait and see, a few days more.*
  There may be something there that
  Wasn't there before.
COGSWORTH: *Perhaps there's something there that*
  Wasn't there before.
MRS. POTTS: *There may be something there that*
  Wasn't there before.

CHIP: What's there, Mama?
MRS. POTTS: Ssh. I'll tell you when you're older.
  Come along, now. Let's give them some privacy . . .

As Belle reads out loud, the Beast marvels that a book can make him forget his troubles. Touched, Belle says she knows how it feels to be different. Downstairs, the Enchanted Objects begin to hope . . .

Human Again . . .

LUMIERE: *I'll be cooking again,*
Be good-looking again,
With a mademoiselle on each arm.
When I'm human again,
Only human again,
Poised and polished and gleaming with charm . . .

LUMIERE: *I'll be courting again.*
Chic and sporting again.
MRS. POTTS: *Which should cause sev'ral husbands alarm!*
CHIP: *I'll hop down off the shelf.*
LUMIERE: *And toute suite be myself.*
CHIP: *I can't wait to be human again!*

MME. DE LA GRANDE BOUCHE/MRS. POTTS/BABETTE:
When we're human again,
Only human again.
When we're knickknacks and whatnots no more.
CHIP: *Little push, little shove,*
They could, whoosh, fall in love.
MME. DE LA GRANDE BOUCHE:
Ah, chérie, won't it all be top-drawer?

MME. DE LA GRANDE BOUCHE:
I'll wear lipstick and rouge,
And I won't be so huge.
Why, I'll easily fit through that door.
I'll exude savoir-faire.
I'll wear gowns! I'll have hair!
It's my prayer to be human again!

COGSWORTH: *When I'm human again,*
Only human again.
When the world once more starts making sense,
I'll unwind for a change.
LUMIERE: *Really? That'd be strange!*
COGSWORTH: *Can I help it if I'm t-t-tense?*

COGSWORTH: *In a shack by the sea,*
I'll sit back sipping tea,

Let my early retirement commence.
Far from fools made of wax,
I'll get down to brass tacks and relax.
ALL: *When I'm human again.*

ALL: *So sweep the dust from the floor!*
Let's let some light in the room!
I can feel, I can tell
Someone might break the spell
Any day now!

LUMIERE/BABETTE: *Shine up the brass on the door!*
Alert the dustpail and broom!
ALL: *If it all goes as planned,*
Our time may be at hand
Any day now!

MRS. POTTS/EGG TIMER/WHISK:
Open the shutters and let in some air.
MRS. POTTS: *Put these here and put those over there.*
ALL: *Sweep up the years*
Of sadness and tears
And throw them away!

ALL: *When we're human again,*
Only human again.
When the girl fin'lly sets us all free,
Cheeks a-bloomin' again,
We're assumin' again
We'll resume our long lost joie de vie.
We'll be playin' again,
Holidayin' again.
And we're prayin' it's A-S-A-P!

When we cast off this pall,
We'll stand straight, we'll walk tall.
When we're all that we were,
Thanks to him, thanks to her.
Coming closer and closer and closer
And closer and . . .

We'll be dancing again!
We'll be twirling again!
We'll be whirling around with such ease.
When we're human again,
Only human again.
We'll go waltzing those old one-two-threes.

We'll be floating again!
We'll be gliding again!
Stepping, striding as fine as you please,
Like a real human does.
I'll be all that I was
On that glorious morn
When we're fin'lly reborn
And we're all of us human again!

Meanwhile, in the tavern, Gaston,
Lefou and a sinister man in black—
Monsieur D'Arque—sit, plotting.

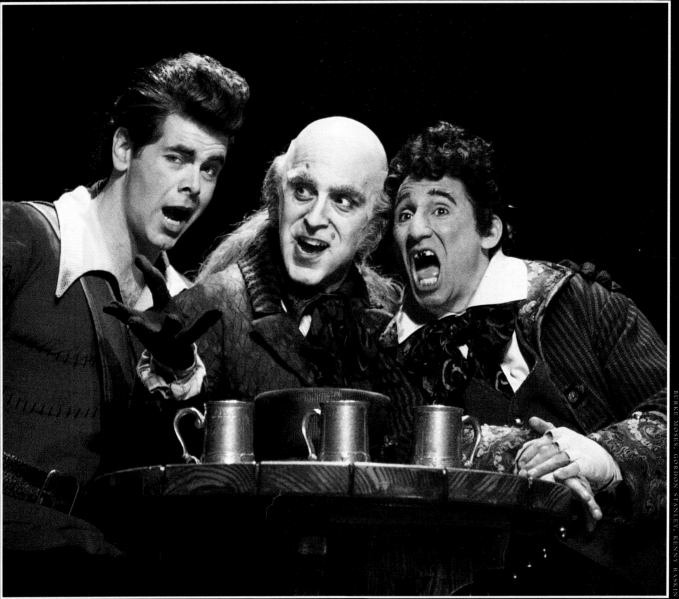

Maison des Lunes . . .

GASTON: *There's a danger I'll be thwarted*
  And denied my honeymoon,
  For the pretty thing I've courted
  Refuses to swoon.
  So, the time has come for a murky plan,
  For which I turn to a murky man.
LEFOU: *To find that fiend*
BOTH: *Where better than*
  The Maison des Lunes?

GASTON: *I don't take this girl for granted.*
  There's no path I haven't hewn
  To her heart; no seed unplanted,
  No flowers unstrewn.
  But quite amazing to relate,
  She doesn't want me for her mate.
LEFOU: *Which forces him to contemplate*
BOTH: *The Maison des Lunes.*

MONSIEUR D'ARQUE: *I don't wish to seem a tad obtuse*
  But I don't see how I can be of use.
  For I lock people up; I'm not a "Lonely Heart's Club."
  I'm a cold, cold fish;
  I've a nasty, vicious streak.
LEFOU: *Please speak!*

GASTON: *It's Belle's father who's your client;*
  She adores the old buffoon.
  She'll be forced to be compliant.
LEFOU: *She'll dance to your tune.*
GASTON: *We get the daughter through her dad.*
  You just pronounce the old boy mad.
LEFOU: *And whoosh! He's slammed up in your pad—*
LEFOU/D'ARQUE: *The Maison des Lunes*

GASTON: *Do I make myself entirely clear?*
D'ARQUE: *It's the simplest deal of my whole foul career!*
GASTON: *Put Maurice away and she'll be here in moments.*
  In a dreadful state
  She'll capitulate to me!
D'ARQUE: *Oh, I'll be strapping up an inmate*
LEFOU: *Very tightly*
GASTON: *Very soon.*
D'ARQUE: *But please don't bring him in late.*
  Our check-in time's noon!
LEFOU/D'ARQUE: *So, wave one bachelor goodbye.*
GASTON: *She'll be my bride.*
LEFOU: *She'd rather die.*
  Than have her daddy ossify?
D'ARQUE: *In my sordid saloon.*
ALL: *So book the church; raise glasses high*
  To the Maison des Lunes!

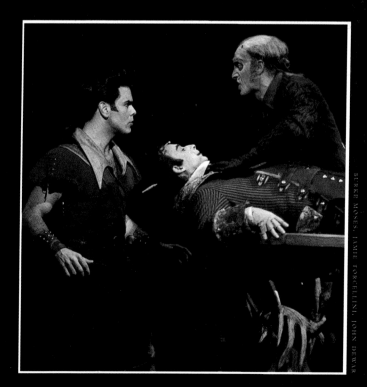

Cogsworth and Lumiere coach the Beast as he dresses for dinner.
With a slight push from Lumiere, the Beast then leads Belle, resplen-
dent in her golden ball gown, down the stairs to the banquet table.

BETH FOWLER

Beauty and the Beast . . .

MRS. POTTS: *Tale as old as time,*
True as it can be.
Barely even friends,
Then somebody bends
Unexpectedly.

Just a little change.
Small, to say the least.
Both a little scared,
Neither one prepared,
Beauty and the Beast.

TERRENCE MANN, SUSAN EGAN

SUSAN EGAN, TERRENCE MANN

SUSAN EGAN, TERRENCE MANN

(Belle asks the Beast to dance.)

MRS. POTTS: *Ever just the same.*
Ever a surprise.
Ever as before,
Ever just as sure
As the sun will rise.

Tale as old as time,
Tune as old as song.
Bittersweet and strange,
Finding you can change,
Learning you were wrong.

Certain as the sun
Rising in the east,
Tale as old as time,
Song as old as rhyme,
Beauty and the Beast.

Tale as old as time,
Song as old as rhyme,
Beauty and the Beast.

SUSAN EGAN

Taking a deep breath, the Beast tries to tell Belle of his feelings,
but he can't find the words. Instead, he gives her his magic mirror,
and in it she sees Maurice struggling. Filled with compassion, the
Beast urges Belle to go to her father. Desperately, he tries to express
his love, but can't. Then Belle is gone, and he is alone . . . forever.

If I Can't Love Her . . .

REPRISE

BEAST: *No spell has been broken,*
No words have been spoken.
No point anymore if she can't love me.
No hope she would do so.
No dream to pursue, so

I finally know that I shall always be
In this hopeless state
And condemned to wait—
Wait for death to set me free.

Monsieur D'Arque and his men arrive to take Maurice away. In a frantic attempt to stop them and to prove Maurice isn't crazy, Belle uses the magic mirror to show the townsfolk the Beast. Everyone gasps. When Belle insists the Beast is really kind, Gaston immediately becomes jealous and whips the crowd into a frenzy.

The Mob Song . . .

MAN 1: *We're not safe until he's dead.*

MAN 2: *He'll come stalking us at night.*

WOMAN: *Set to sacrifice our children*
  To his monstrous appetite.

MAN 3: *He'll wreak havoc on our village*
  If we let him wander free.

GASTON: *So, it's time to take action, boys.*
  It's time to follow me.

GASTON: *Through the mist, through the wood.*
  Through the darkness and the shadows.
  It's a nightmare, but it's one exciting ride!
  Say a prayer, then we're there,
  At the drawbridge of a castle
  And there's something truly terrible inside.

'SKIP HARRIS   ARLENE THOMAS   RICK SPAANS   SUZI CARR GEORGE   KEN MCMULLEN   LINDA GRIFFIN   MICHAEL PATERNOSTO

It's a beast! He's got fangs,
Razor sharp ones!
Massive paws, killer claws for the feast.
Hear him roar! See him foam!
But we're not coming home 'til he's dead—
Good and dead! Kill the beast!

(Gaston and the mob move through the forest.)

MOB: *Light your torch, mount your horse!*
GASTON: *Screw your courage to the sticking place!*
MOB: *We're counting on Gaston to lead the way!*
MOB WOMEN: *Through a mist, through a wood,*
Where within a haunted castle
Something's lurking that you don't see ev'ryday!

MOB: *It's a beast! One as tall as a mountain.*
We won't rest 'til he's good and deceased.
Sally forth! Tally ho!
Grab your sword! Grab your bow!
Praise the Lord and here we go!

We don't like what we don't understand.
In fact, it scares us.
And this monster is mysterious, at least.

Bring your guns! Bring your knives!
Save your children and your wives!
We'll save our village and our lives.
We'll kill the beast!

(The crowd cuts down a tree to storm the castle.)

MOB: *Hearts ablaze, banners high,*
We go marching into battle,
Unafraid, although the danger's just increased.

Raise the flag! Sing the song!
Here we come, we're fifty strong!
And fifty Frenchmen can't be wrong!
Let's kill the beast! (Boom!)
Kill the beast! (Boom!)
Kill the beast! (Crash!)
Kill the beast!

While the Enchanted Objects trounce the mob, Gaston taunts the dejected Beast and tries to stab him. Then Belle runs in, shouting "No!," and the Beast grabs Gaston, dangling him over the turret. But the Beast is too human to kill Gaston; instead, he pulls Gaston up and orders him to get out. As the Beast turns, arms outstretched, toward Belle, Gaston plunges a knife into his back. The Beast staggers, bumping into Gaston, who falls off the turret, to his death. Gasping, the Beast collapses into Belle's arms.

Transformation . . .

BELLE: *We are home.*
   We are where we shall be forever.
   Trust in me,
   For you know I won't run away.
   From today,
   This is all that I need,
   And all that I need to say is . . .

   Home should be where the heart is.
   I'm certain as I can be
   I found home.
   You're my home.
   Stay with me.

("Don't leave me. I love you," Belle sobs as the last rose petal falls. The Beast then rises into the air, spinning around, and is transformed into the Prince.)

PRINCE: *Belle, look into my eyes!*
   Belle, don't you recognize
   The beast within the man
   Who's here before you?
BELLE: *It is you!*

(The Prince and Belle finally kiss . . . and, suddenly, everyone is human again. Overwhelmed with joy, Cogsworth embraces Lumiere, and Chip runs into his mother's arms. The Prince and Belle begin to dance.)

77

SUSAN EGAN,
TERRENCE MANN

BELLE/PRINCE: *Two lives have begun now!*
  Two hearts become one now!
  One passion, one dream.
  One thing forever true:
  I love you!

Beauty and the Beast . . .
REPRISE

ALL: *Certain as the sun*
  Rising in the east,
  Tale as old as time,
  Song as old as rhyme,
  Beauty and the Beast.

  Tale as old as time,
  Song as old as rhyme,
  Beauty and the Beast.

(The curtain falls.)

PART TWO

The Characters

Belle

Belle is a star even before she appears on stage, for many in the audience already adore this character from the animated feature. Recognizing this love, costume designer Ann Hould-Ward dressed Belle in her familiar blue outfit but embellished it with rich details, using silky fabrics, delicate patterning, touches of lace, and intricate embroidery.

From the opening song, Belle comes across as special. Here is a spirited beauty who enjoys reading and is truly excited at the way books open up a new world of adventure and possibility. "We felt strongly about making her an intelligent woman—woman, not girl—-who could be accepted as a good role model," explains scriptwriter Linda Woolverton. "At the same time,

she has to have the qualities of a fairy-tale heroine. She must be elevated through her deeds."

It was no easy task to find an actress who could bring Belle to life on stage, making her believable in person. "We looked not for the traditional sweet ingenue but for someone with a tremendous sense of adventure and spine," says casting director Jay Binder. "Belle has a lot of determination; she really is the moral conscience of the play."

At the auditions for the initial cast, actress Susan Egan surprised everyone with her fresh insights into the character. As Egan has underlined to reporters, "Belle's gutsy. . . . She's not a damsel in distress. She can save herself, thank you very much!"

In rehearsals Egan, like Belle, didn't hesitate to speak out if she thought the script was off. Every line, every action, she felt, had to be believable as something Belle would say or do. Why, for example, Egan wondered, would Belle run away from the castle after promising to stay? The Beast must have done more than roar in rage, Egan reasoned; Belle must have felt her life

was being threatened. To make this clear, the script was changed, and the Beast now grabs at Belle and accidentally tears off her sleeve.

If Belle's curiosity gets her into trouble in the West Wing, her openness to new ideas and her honest perceptiveness allow her to fall in love with the Beast. "Belle makes a transition," producer Robert McTyre points out. "As strong as she is at the beginning, she still grows up during the play and learns to see beyond the Beast's outward ugliness."

Belle's costumes become more and more beautiful, reflecting her growing love for the Beast. Her two yellow gowns recall the splendor of the French court in the mid- to late 1700s. "To me," says Hould-Ward, "Belle's

elaborate gowns are a gift of how I wish my daughter's life could be and I don't think any woman's life really is today. They represent a romantic fantasy, and while that fantasy is not reality, it can be a wonderful place to go to for an hour or two in the theater."

For Egan the ball gown creates its own magic, even though it weighs over 40 pounds. On nights when she is tired, she remembers that this is the dress she dreamed of wearing when she was 10 years old. And she knows that in the audience there are little girls wearing their own versions of this yellow dress. Some nights when she walks out on stage, she can even hear a little girl say, "She looks just like me!"

Beast

Trapped in a hulking, hairy body, with huge clawed hands and sharply pointed horns, the Beast must somehow win the heart of Belle as well as the audience. To Terrence Mann, who created the role for the stage, the story of the Beast is about a young boy who made a horrible mistake when he turned away the old beggar woman. Mann describes how the Beast feels regret for his action and an overwhelming shame at his terrifying visage. "If only I hadn't made that mistake," the Beast thinks, "everything would be different"—a feeling, Mann suggests, to which many people can relate.

To make the idea of a human "beast" more believable to a theater audience, director Robert Jess Roth drew inspiration from rock performers. "In the movie," he explains, "the Beast has a cuddly, teddy-bear-like quality underneath his rough exterior. But for a live performance, we needed more chemistry between Belle and the Beast. I wanted the Beast to show his chest and have long hair, to create an animalistic magnetism on stage."

The final appearance of the Beast derives from many sources. Costume designer Ann Hould-Ward began by looking at the animated version and then moved on to pictures of werewolves and beasts through the ages, in fairy tales, films, and television

programs, as well as photos of rock musicians. Fueled by this research and by her conversations with others about their images of beasts, Hould-Ward sketched dozens of possibilities. Then, to fine-tune her ideas, she observed Mann's interpretation of the Beast in rehearsals.

There was never any question that Mann, who had played Rum Tum Tugger in *Cats* and Javert in *Les Misérables,* would be convincing as the menacing yet endearing Beast. "He brings so much depth to the role, so much humanity, coupled with his amazing ability to physicalize the role and make the audience believe that he is both an animal and a man at the same time," says casting director Jay Binder.

Mann believes the physicality of the role forces him to stay focused. "A part of this character is about staying calm and then exploding . . . and that's hard to do unless you're focused," he explained to one reporter.

For both Mann and scriptwriter Linda Woolverton, it was a challenge to hint at the Beast's potential eloquence despite his gruff manner, to make the audience believe that this frightening creature could express the passionate feelings of the song "If I Can't Love Her." As Woolverton explains, "When I first heard Alan Menken (the composer) play the song, I knew that I had to make sure the Beast evolved naturally into a character

96

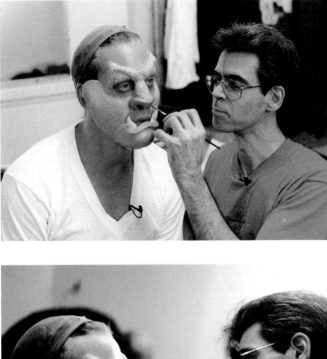

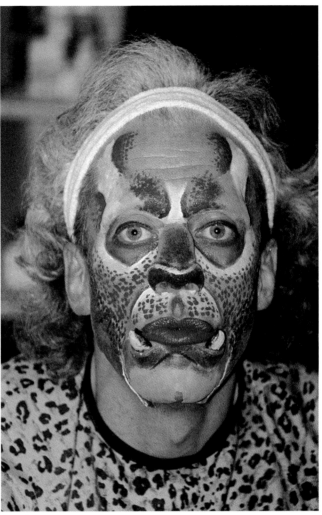

who could sing such an emotionally powerful song. I still cry every time I hear his song." She began elevating the Beast's language slightly, so that he moves beyond blunt, angry retorts and tries, in his words, "to act like a gentle man." To give the audience a brief glimpse of his inner turmoil, Menken and lyricist Tim Rice added another, short number, "How Long Must This Go On?," which Rice describes as "a prelude to his soul-searching ballad."

Many changes were made in the Beast's makeup to permit his emotions to come through. "Initially, the Beast had masses of rubber on his face that we gradually, inch by inch, removed to let the audience see Terrence Mann's expressions," says prosthetics expert John Dods. "He still has a rubber nose, a rubber lower lip piece, rubber fangs, rubber eyebrows, and rubber cheek pieces, but they're thinner and smaller than they were at first; his face has less hair and more skin is exposed. There's no longer

a barricade between Mann's acting and the audience."

In addition to the rubber pieces on his face, Mann wears gloves with painted latex claws and bestial rubber toes, which are glued to the outside of his boots. The Beast's chest and abdomen are also rubber pieces, covered with hair that has been permed to create a wild look. The abdomen is edged with a special lightweight hair "cloth," woven out of hair on a unique loom and then groomed by hair designer David H. Lawrence. Originally, Lawrence used 20 pounds of human and yak hair for the Beast's look, although he gradually decreased the amount, making the costume more comfortable for the actor.

Even with all the changes, the Beast's costume is hot. As Mann remarked to one reporter, "It's like putting on my heaviest winter coat and running around the block in springtime for two hours." But that doesn't lessen his enthusiasm for the show. To Mann, it is simply "magical."

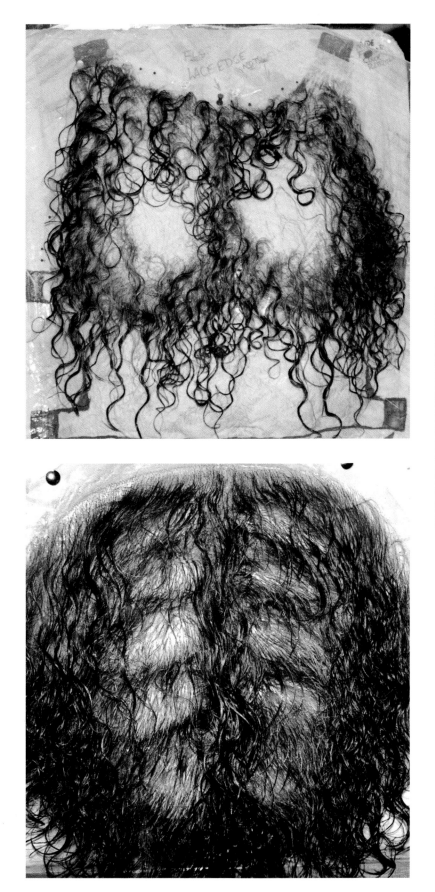

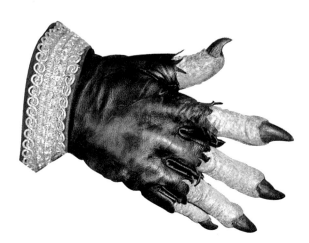

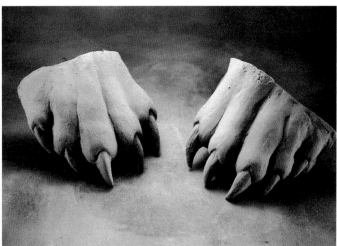

Maurice

As soon as Maurice arrives on stage atop his invention—boom—it explodes and he tumbles off. A few minutes later, when Belle asks her father if he thinks she's odd, he answers from behind his machine, "My daughter! Odd?" Immediately he pops up, wearing a most unusual helmet and huge goggles, and inquires, "Now where would you get an idea like that?" The picture of a good-natured but scatterbrained inventor is established.

Yet Maurice is also a loving father, as his duet with Belle, "No Matter What," makes clear. "With this song," says lyricist Tim Rice, "we took the opportunity to expand Maurice's character and to emphasize the love between father and daughter."

To underline Maurice's importance as Belle's father, casting director Jay Binder initially looked for someone who would be immediately recognizable as the quintessential father. Tom Bosley, well known to American audiences for his starring role as Mr. C. in the television series *Happy Days*, was the perfect choice. "In addition to comic ability," Binder stresses, "the actor playing Maurice has to convey a tremendous amount of warmth."

Costume designer Ann Hould-Ward also wanted to make sure Maurice was instantly identifiable on stage. "With each of the principal characters," she explains, "it was important to start off with an outfit that related to the animated film. They need to be introduced in the clothes worn in the animation, but after the first appearance, you can go on to other clothes that might be in the characters' closets."

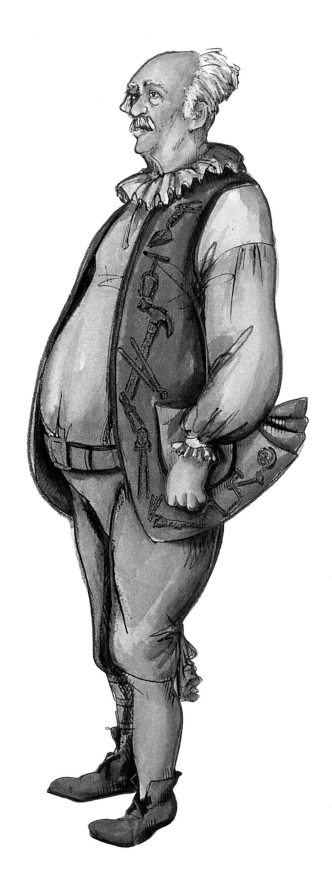

Drawing on the touch of looniness in Maurice's character, Hould-Ward added playful patterns to his shirt and vest. And, of course, she made sure his stockings never matched.

One costume that Hould-Ward sketched, but never used, was Maurice in his nightshirt and stocking cap. It's just what you'd expect him to wear if you caught sight of him toddling off to bed.

Gaston

The villain of the story is Gaston, who is just the opposite of the Beast. "The Beast is someone with a beastly exterior and a human interior," explains scriptwriter Linda Woolverton. "In contrast, Gaston has a handsome exterior and a beastly interior. As the story evolves, the two switch places—the Beast becomes more human, and Gaston's beastly nature is revealed."

Casting the role was difficult. "The actor must be young, tall, and handsome with an impressive physique," says producer Robert McTyre. "He must be not only a good actor but also an amusing

comedian and a wonderful singer. How many people have all those qualities?"

For the initial cast, Burke Moses was a perfect choice, convincing the audience the moment he swaggers on stage. Moses loves playing the part, pointing out, "Gaston acts in the way we all want to act but can't. Everybody wants to have a little swagger now and then—unfortunately, he has it all the time!"

In his interpretation Moses wanted to honor the film. "The animated character moves very dynamically, like a superhero in a comic book," he indicates, "so I tried to make my movements equally dynamic. I see Gaston as part peacock and part hunter. At times I point my toe in an almost feminine balletic movement and at other times I stalk, like a predator, across the stage."

As Moses points out, "Gaston definitely makes a distinct impression on the audience," and he credits much of that impact to the work of the writer, composer, and lyricists. "They created a very straightforward, simple character. The most complex thing in the world of theater is to create something simple."

BURKE MOSES, SUSAN EGAN

Cogsworth

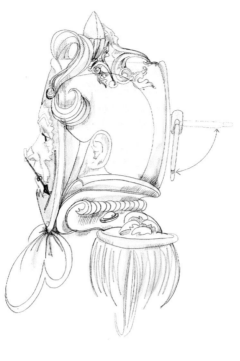

With his British-sounding name, Cogsworth calls to mind the meticulous, ever-so-proper head butler. His transformation into a mantel clock is a delightful pun on his personality, for with each appearance he becomes, in Lumiere's words, "a little more tightly wound . . . a little more ticked off!" At the same time his nervous fussiness is an all-too-human foible. When a huge winding key appears on his back and he cries out at the loss of dignity, his plight evokes both laughter and sympathy.

To portray Cogsworth on the Broadway stage, actor Heath Lamberts drew on his background in farce, but most important, he says, "I brought all the believability and honesty I could to the role."

At times Lamberts found his costume constraining, especially in an early version (later changed) in which his head was totally encased in his helmet.

Eventually, he learned to take advantage of these restrictions to demonstrate just how a human clock might move. "Cogsworth's little waddle comes out of the one freedom I had—which was to move sideways," says Lamberts.

Lamberts underlines how helpful and encouraging the other actors were when he encountered difficulties with his role. On a certain level he compares the way he came to terms with his performance to the lesson Cogsworth himself learns during the course of the play. "Cogsworth is very self-consumed at first," Lamberts suggests, "but he finds that it is only through the intervention and assistance of others that his goals are achieved—it's a call to gratitude." At the end of the show, when he excitedly kisses Lumiere over and over again, we know Cogsworth has truly changed.

Lumiere

Offsetting Cogsworth, the consummate English butler, is
Lumiere, the dashing, debonair, ever-so-French valet. The
original character in the animated film was inspired by the
French singer and actor Maurice Chevalier, an influence that
is clearly acknowledged when Lumiere, complete with hat and
cane, suavely invites Belle to "Be Our Guest."

The name Lumiere, French for "light," truly describes the
character, according to actor Gary Beach, a Broadway veteran.
"He is romantic, and he is also the light (both literally and

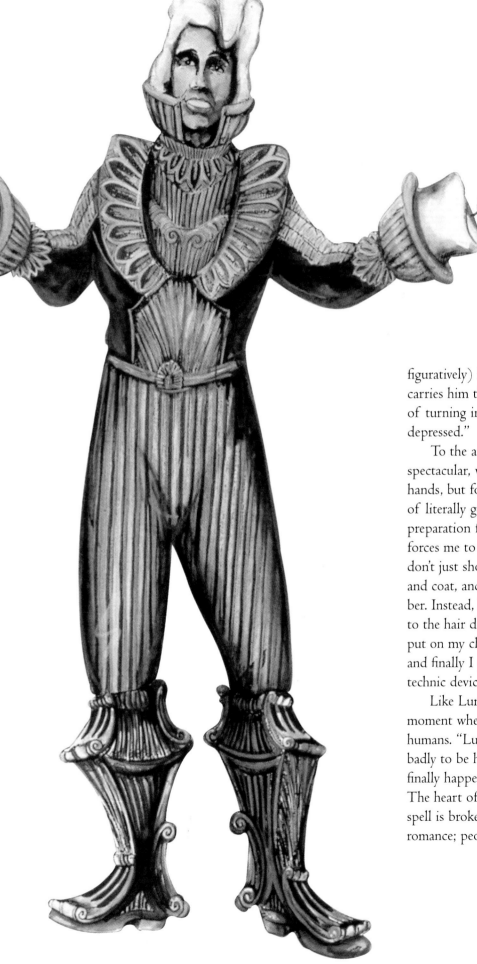

figuratively) in the castle. His optimism carries him through this terrible ordeal of turning into a candlestick. He's never depressed."

To the audience Lumiere's costume is spectacular, with actual butane flames as hands, but for Beach the costume is a way of literally getting into his character. "The preparation for each performance physically forces me to concentrate," he claims. "I don't just show up, slip on a pair of slacks and coat, and run on stage to do my number. Instead, I first do my makeup; then I go to the hair department for my wig; then I put on my clothes, boots, and microphone; and finally I get into my 'arms,' the pyrotechnic device. It's very methodical."

Like Lumiere, Beach treasures the moment when the servants turn into humans. "Lumiere and the others want so badly to be humans," he says, "that when it finally happens, the audience often cheers. The heart of the show is really that the spell is broken. There's more than the romance; people are fulfilling themselves."

Mrs. Potts & Chip

The counterpart to Maurice, Belle's father, is Mrs. Potts, the Beast's surrogate mother. As her rounded teapot form suggests, she represents warm, cozy comfort. And almost everywhere she goes, she takes along her perky little boy, Chip, transformed into a teacup.

Veteran Broadway actress Beth Fowler underlines Mrs. Potts's maternal qualities: "Caretaking is her whole reason for being, and she does it practically and simply, with love and in the spirit of giving. To me, she is the quintessential mother, offering love, warmth, security, nurturing, feeding—all those things."

BETH FOWLER,
BRIAN PRESS

Although her costume is confining, Fowler doesn't mind the constraints. "As Mrs. Potts, I don't *want* to move like a real person," she points out, "so the costume actually helps me portray the character. I'm not playing a teapot, but a mother who has been transformed into a teapot." As designer Ann Hould-Ward intended, the costume gives the actress a way into that experience performance after performance.

To the audience, the most confining "costume" belongs to Chip (played by Brian Press for the initial show). His body has magically disappeared, leaving only his head for us to see. The illusion heightens the drama, for through the actor's subtle head movements and changes in facial expression and tone of voice, Chip's bubbling energy comes through. Will this exuberant child remain imprisoned by the spell? Like Mrs. Potts, we want to see him run through the castle again.

Babette

From her very first words, "Oooh-la-la," Babette (originated by actress Stacey Logan) is the epitome of the saucy French coquette. She literally "tickles" Lumiere's fancy with her fluffy, feather-duster hands. The pair's lighthearted flirtation is full of fun, intro-ducing a playful spirit to the dark and gloomy castle.

Babette's streamlined costume, elegantly ruffled with plumes, accentuates her curvaceous allure. Human again, as a maid, her pertness is echoed in the sweep of her low-cut neckline and the flounce of her skirt.

Madame de la Grande Bouche

Madame de la Grande Bouche is truly of operatic proportions, adding humor on stage. In her moment of glory as a Wagnerian Brunhilde during the mob scene, she stuns Lefou with her high C.

Madame de la Grande Bouche's costume guarantees her magnificence. She has drawers that actually open and an ornate headpiece studded with jewels. Actress Eleanor Glockner, who originated the role, could feel a burden being lifted off her shoulders as the designers lightened the weight of her headpiece, using vacuformed material, hollow jewels, and cotton balls that were coated to look like pearls.

123

Lefou

Short and clownishly stupid, Lefou is Gaston's loyal sidekick. Always eager to please his idol, he cheerfully springs back from Gaston's constant punches.

Beyond comic ability, the part of Lefou (originated by Kenny Raskin) calls for acrobatic talent. Even though his costume is fully padded to soften any blows, Lefou still has to know just how to tumble. And he doesn't miss a beat when the Doormat grabs him in the castle and they cartwheel in tandem across the stage.

KENNY RASKIN

Silly Girls

LINDA TALCOTT, PAIGE PRICE, SARAH SOLI SHANNON

Giggling and fluttering around Gaston, the Silly Girls live up to their name. From their frilly costumes to their tittering voices, they present a complete contrast to Belle.

Enchantress

The gnarled old beggar woman suddenly turns into a glistening Enchantress, who flies up, above the stage. Her flowing hair sparkles with many different strands of color. "She's our stained-glass window," says hair designer David H. Lawrence, referring to the beautiful window in the opening of the animated feature.

Enchanted Objects

As they sing and dance on stage, the Enchanted Objects are also visually entertaining. Every detail on their costumes deserves a closer look, from the cupped feet of the Egg Timer to the gleaming silverware bands atop each Napkin Ring's head.

With each costume, designer Ann Hould-Ward and her assistants took care to use light-weight materials, such as specially molded plastic, for the actors' comfort. During rehearsals Hould-Ward fine-tuned her designs to make sure each actor could move with relative ease. When, for example, the Cheese Grater's headpiece interfered with his arm movement, she trimmed a bit off the top.

BILL NAVEL

ANNA MCNEELY

KIM HUBER

ELMORE JAMES

BARBARA MARINEAU

DEREK SPAANS

IVY FOX

MERWIN FOARD

GORDON STANLEY

Monsieur D'Arque

Clothed in somber colors, with a
Scrooge-like hat and cape, Monsieur
D'Arque is every inch the villain.

Townsfolk

In the opening scene the townsfolk are dressed in
bright colors and cheerfully greet each other:
"Bonjour!" Later, though, when they gather around
Gaston, shouting "Kill the Beast," they are garbed in
dark colors and appear much less friendly.

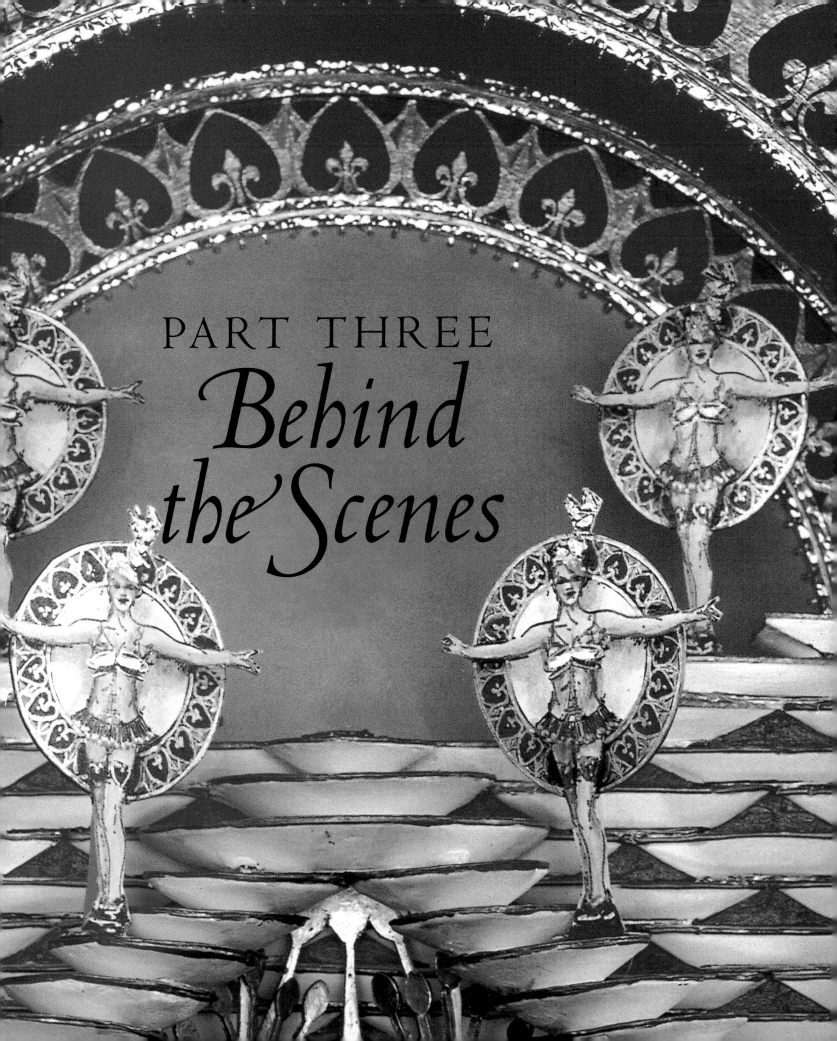

PART THREE

Behind the Scenes

$\mathcal{F}$OR CENTURIES, THE STORY OF BEAUTY
and the Beast has enchanted children and adults all over the world. It is truly a
"tale as old as time," rooted in ancient legends from Greece, India, and Africa.
This endearing love story became especially popular in the French court of the
mid-eighteenth century, and the best-known written version was published in
1756 by Madame le Prince de Beaumont.

Over the years Beaumont's story was adapted in children's books, poems,
plays, and film. Then, in the late 1980s, the Walt Disney Company decided to
animate this powerful fairy tale. Executives Michael Eisner, Roy E. Disney, Frank
Wells, and Jeffrey Katzenberg all agreed that *Beauty and the Beast* was one of the
greatest love stories ever told and a natural successor to such Disney animation
classics as *Snow White and the Seven Dwarfs, Cinderella,* and *Sleeping Beauty.*

Writer Linda Woolverton, lyricist Howard Ashman, composer Alan
Menken, producer Don Hahn, and directors Kirk Wise and Gary Trousdale
made major revisions in the fairy tale to bring it to life on the screen. Belle
(French for "Beauty") stands out as a heroine for the nineties—not just beautiful
and virtuous, but also smart and strong-willed, unafraid to challenge the Beast.
She is tormented not by wicked sisters, as in the original story, but by an out-
wardly handsome suitor—Gaston—who is truly a beast inside. The biggest
change, however, occurs inside the Beast's castle. Instead of being left alone with
the Beast, Belle is entertained by servants who have been transformed by the spell
into household objects. Singing and dancing, a teapot-cook, clock-butler, cande-
labra-valet, and many others weave their own spell of fun and enchantment.

Released in 1991, Disney's *Beauty and the Beast* garnered widespread critical
acclaim. It was the first animated feature to be nominated for an Academy Award
for Best Picture and received two Oscars, for Best Original Musical Score and
Best Song (for the evocative title ballad). Everybody raved about the music. Frank
Rich, theater critic of the *New York Times,* pointed out that the best musical score
of the year wasn't on Broadway, it was in Disney's film *Beauty and the Beast.*

On to Broadway

"For a long time we had been considering a theatrical presence on Broadway,"
recalls Michael Eisner, Walt Disney Company chairman. "*Beauty and the Beast*
seemed the perfect choice for our first venture. Even when they were performed
on their own, without any staging or costumes, the songs held the attention of an
audience. But there were two major hurdles in bringing the animated feature to
the stage: How could we make the Enchanted Objects believable in a live performance, and how could we retain the magic of the Beast's transformation?"

OPPOSITE:
*Seen side by side, Ann Hould-Ward's
costume sketches suggest visually how
the handsome Prince could turn into
the frightening Beast. The Prince's
flowing ponytail, for example, becomes
an unruly mane, and his whole body
thickens into a hulking presence.
Horns sprout from his head, hair
covers his face, and clawed toes
emerge from the tips of his boots.*

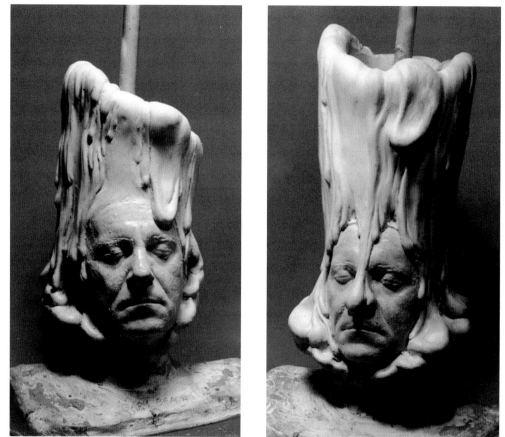

Eisner called Ron Logan and Robert McTyre, president and vice president of Walt Disney Theatrical Productions, who gathered people together to develop ideas. The team of director Robert Jess Roth, scenic designer Stan Meyer, concept writer Tom Child, and choreographer Matt West, who had collaborated on several successful Disney theme park productions, soon came up with a new twist to the story: When the Enchantress places the spell on the castle, the servants don't immediately turn into objects, as in the film; instead, they at first appear more human and slowly transform into objects as the petals fall off the rose.

Scene by scene, Roth, Meyer, and West outlined how the 85-minute film could be adapted for a two-and-a-half-hour Broadway show. "We looked for places where new songs could be added," indicates Roth. "And every one of the songs we spotted then is in the show now. The songs themselves have changed a lot, but the places where they come and who sings them have remained about the same."

Now it was time to add some magic. Associate producer Donald Frantz brought in Jim Steinmeyer and John Gaughan, who had created illusions for such leading magicians as David Copperfield and Doug Henning. Frantz also turned to costume designer Ann Hould-Ward, who had proved she could recreate fairy-tale characters on stage and remain faithful to an original artwork with her wonderful designs for *Into the Woods* and *Sunday in the Park with George.*

Armed with costume sketches, two illusion prototypes, and about 140 story-boards, the team convinced Michael Eisner and Jeffrey Katzenberg, then chairman of Walt Disney Studios, to go ahead with the project. The next step was to bring in members of the original *Beauty and the Beast* team: writer Linda Woolverton and composer Alan Menken, as well as lyricist Tim Rice, who worked with Menken on *Aladdin* after Howard Ashman died and who wrote the lyrics for the Broadway shows *Joseph and the Amazing Technicolor Dreamcoat, Jesus Christ Superstar, Evita,* and *Chess.*

"When I first heard of the project, I thought it was impossible, because the movie was so good," admits Rice. "But when I saw what they had in mind, I realized that this could be a wonderful, traditional but contemporary Broadway show."

A period of intense collaboration followed, with everyone talking to each other and excitedly exchanging ideas. The goal was not simply to translate, but to reinvent the animated feature for Broadway. "We were walking a line," explains Menken. "We wanted it to feel both familiar and brand new. And we had to be sure something was gained dramatically by bringing it to the stage."

The key lay in the power of the story itself. "Above all, *Beauty and the Beast* is a moving love story, which we wanted to make a dramatic emotional experience for the audience," says producer Robert McTyre. The emphasis was on portraying the true love between Belle and the Beast, as well as the poignant wish of the Enchanted Objects to be human again.

There is a clear relationship between the fluffy little cap of the human Mrs. Potts (left) and the broader, stiffer top of Mrs. Potts, the teapot (right).

OVERLEAF:

Expanding on his black-and-white storyboard sketches (see the endpapers for examples), Stan Meyer did seven detailed drawings in color to show how the drama would unfold on stage.

As the show moved into rehearsals and previews at Houston's Theatre Under the Stars, Eisner was there, offering suggestions and encouragement. At times the creative team was holding on to an element from the movie that just didn't work on stage. "Take it out," Eisner urged. "Although you need to retain the essence of the movie," he told the creators, "this is a different production. It has to be able to succeed as a theatrical experience."

The first night of previews in New York demonstrated how powerful that live theater experience can be. At the penultimate moment in the fight scene, with the rain pouring and the lightning flashing, as the Beast turned away from Gaston to reach toward Belle, and Gaston rose, knife in hand—suddenly, from the middle of the mezzanine, a seven-year-old boy's voice cried out, "No!"

Seeing live actors intensifies the drama. "I can watch it every night," says New York stage manager Jim Harker, "and still get choked up when the objects are transformed—which will always be the case, because it's connected with a real person." That's the magic of theater.

A Commitment to Theater

"The theater experience is an extremely important part of our culture," Michael Eisner maintains. "People are social beings; they want to go out—which is why we at Disney are making more and more of a commitment to live entertainment."

As *Beauty and the Beast* continued to delight audiences on Broadway, Disney began mounting separate shows in Los Angeles and Toronto, as well as a touring production. They also licensed the musical to companies in Japan, Australia, Austria, and other countries. With every new staging, they reexamined the production, changing details to heighten the drama and make it glow in the particular theater.

"We are bringing a new way of thinking to the theater," says producer Robert McTyre, "both creatively and businesswise. On the creative end, the show is a very collaborative effort, with many more people involved and contributing than usual. And, on the business side, we bring financial discipline. Most important, we're developing new audiences, stimulating people—children and adults—to fall in love with the theater."

Directing a Team

Everybody emphasizes the unusual collaboration that underlies the success of *Beauty and the Beast*. The script, music, costumes, sets, lighting, acting, choreography, and technical wizardry—none of these stands off on its own, isolated from the rest. Everything is fully integrated into the whole, which is the result of a constant give-and-take between all the members of the creative team.

Director Robert Jess Roth already knew the value of collaboration, for he had worked closely for several years with Stan Meyer and Matt West. His job was to field everybody's input into a cohesive vision. "As a director," he stresses, "you don't need to have all the ideas; instead, you need to listen to your collaborators' ideas and give everything a fair hearing. It's a partnership."

Roth underlines the inspiration provided by Michael Eisner and Jeffrey Katzenberg: "They had very different kinds of notes. Michael's tended to be larger in scope: things to do with the overall tone of a scene or song. Jeffrey's notes were always very specific, detailed and numerous. This combination of notes was a tremendous help to the show and to me personally. The actors were also a great source of inspiration in helping us develop the emotional heart of the story."

Roth never had any doubts about where the emphasis of the production should be. "Although much has been made of the spectacle, the show works because of the emotional heart of the story," he insists. "Everybody can relate to it in one way or another."

Elaborating the Story

For writer Linda Woolverton, "At first the idea of reworking the script was hard because I had spent three years on the movie. But it turned out to be a wonderful experience. I wasn't struggling with telling the story and I already knew the characters, so I could just *play*. I could develop Belle and the Beast's relationship and define the common ground between them. There was also a new vision for the Enchanted Objects. In the show Cogsworth, Lumiere, Mrs. Potts, and the others are becoming progressively more and more like objects, so they have a stake in Belle and the Beast coming together. You have more empathy for them."

Woolverton's favorite moment is the library scene, when Belle introduces the Beast to the magic of books, by reading him the story of King Arthur. "In a concise way," she says, "this scene clarifies why Belle and the Beast can connect. I was happy to find a way to do it small, without overloading it with words."

The art of simplifying the story and bringing out the underlying emotion in every scene is something she learned from lyricist Howard Ashman while working with him on the animated feature. "I got the education of a lifetime from Howard," she reflects. "Now I don't look at a script or a scene without asking, 'What would Howard think?'"

In collaborating with the lyricists, Woolverton stresses that they all had to have the same sense of the voice of the character. At first she'd write the dialogue leading up to the song moment, but after hearing the lyrics, she often reworked the script to flow seamlessly into the song. "Essentially," she indicates, "it's my job to take the characters to the place where the music emerges from them naturally, as if they had no other choice but to start singing."

Through the rehearsals and previews, the script went through many changes. "What I love about live theater," exclaims Woolverton, "is that you can just *try* a new line; you can put it in and see if it works for the audience." And even when the script is finalized, the play is never static. "Every night is different," says Woolverton. "Every line reading, every interpretation of the actor is slightly different. That's the excitement of live theater."

Expanding the Score

Flowing through the performance is the music. From the beginning, when writing the score for the animated feature, says composer Alan Menken, "Howard Ashman and I structured it as a stage musical. We wanted each song to push the

From an initial sketch (top), Cogsworth's headgear evolved into an elaborate helmet (center), although only the simpler version (bottom) was finally used.

OPPOSITE AND OVERLEAF:
Stan Meyer changed the design of the castle garden for different scenes and different productions. In Los Angeles he created a romantic moonlit landscape (opposite top) for when Belle dances with the Beast. Then, for the finale, he used a colorful daylit screen, which appears behind a hanger (overleaf) with cherubs coming to life and garlands of roses in full bloom. For Toronto, Meyer painted the architecture onto a backdrop where the sun is rising (opposite bottom).

plot forward. Our characters sing about their thoughts and feelings, telling the story. It's entirely musical theater."

In transferring the songs from the film to the stage, Menken felt very protective of the lyrics written by the late Howard Ashman, for the two had worked together for many years on such acclaimed stage musicals as *God Bless You, Mr. Rosewater* and *Little Shop of Horrors*, as well as the award-winning Disney animations *The Little Mermaid, Beauty and the Beast*, and *Aladdin* (Ashman died before completing the latter). Yet Menken also wanted to reinvigorate the songs, "to shake them up enough so everything feels fresh." So, for example, in "Be Our Guest" and "Gaston," he added a few lyrics that Ashman had written but were not used in the film, such as the line "Who can make up these endless refrains like Gaston?"

Working with lyricist Tim Rice, orchestrator Danny Troob, music supervisor Michael Kosarin, and vocal arranger David Friedman, Menken tried to expand the score in a way that was seamless with the original. To flesh out the story on stage, six major new songs, as well as several shorter musical numbers, were added. "We looked for moments that cried out for song," notes Menken. "When Belle says to Gaston, 'What do you know about my dreams?' and he answers, 'Plenty,' launching into a reverie of how their life will be—that clearly signals a song in musical theater terms. When Belle is taken to her room and the doors close, we can finally have Belle's solo moment. And when the Beast drives Belle away and then realizes what he has done, there is a compelling dramatic reason for a passionate song."

The new songs help establish the characters, giving the audience a chance to know them more fully. "Both 'Home' and 'If I Can't Love Her' deal with aspects of the story already implicit in the movie but not dealt with at length," Rice indicates. "'Home' deals with Belle's feelings of hopelessness when she is first imprisoned by the Beast, and 'If I Can't Love Her' reveals the Beast's desperation as he faces up to imprisonment of a different kind."

A peak moment in the show is when the Enchanted Objects sing "Human Again," which was originally written by Ashman and Menken for the film but not used. On stage, the song has found its rightful place, for as we watch the servants become more and more objectlike, we too want them to be human again.

A particularly poignant song, both in the film and on stage, is "Beauty and the Beast," sung by Mrs. Potts as Belle and the Beast dance together. Menken credits the power of this song to the emotional simplicity of Ashman's lyrics. Beth Fowler, who created the role of Mrs. Potts for Broadway, admits, "Often I'm fighting back tears when I sing 'Beauty and the Beast.' It's a very touching moment. And the song makes me feel good every night. It's a gift to get to sing that song."

Designing the Sets

Working on a production with such powerful music delighted scenic designer Stan Meyer. "The music evokes a strong emotional response," says Meyer, "which affects the way I envision the scenery."

But before he could even begin designing the sets Meyer faced an incredible

LINE OF
BACKING

OPEN

The blueprint for the castle interior shows different architectural styles. "It is an enchanted castle," explains Meyer, "so there's no reason it can't be a mixture of architectural periods—gothic, baroque, rococo, and empire—all coming together to make a castle that seems monumental in scale."

6"

1'-1"

5'-4"   3'-0"   ~3 RECESSED PANELS

1'-3"

SIDE

LEVATIONS

challenge. When he went through the original movie script with director Roth and choreographer West, he sketched the various scenes and soon accumulated a stack of over 50 different locations. "There was no way we could have so many different sets!" he exclaims. "We didn't have the space to store all the scenery. Besides, we wanted to do a *theatrical* production, not a repeat of the movie, and that necessitated making some very different choices."

Although an animated feature can quickly shift from place to place to place, on stage the sets must be actually, physically, moved. In fact, part of the magic of good theater is to create the illusion of many different scenes from just a few basic sets. Take the inside of the Beast's castle, for example. "Rather than build dozens of different castle sets," Meyer explains, "we simply move smaller scenic pieces—adding a table and chairs, bringing in swags, or shifting the columns—to change the space. And, of course, we alter the lighting. In this way the same basic set can become a hallway, Belle's room, the library, a dining room—whatever we need it to be."

Roth and Meyer worked hard to create a smooth flow to the staging, with one scene moving easily into the next. "We don't bring down the curtain or go to blackout—unless there's a strong dramatic reason for doing so," Meyer indicates. For example, when the Beast roars at Maurice, "I'll give you a place to stay," a blackout punctuates the tension, and then the music plays and takes you to another scene.

As he designed, Meyer analyzed the characters and envisioned the live actors inhabiting his spaces. He was delighted when actors later told him they felt at home in his sets. At times Meyer created deliberate juxtapositions between the character and the set. In the tavern, for example, the very masculine but warm and inviting environment contrasts with the essentially cold, self-centered persona of Gaston. A different contrast is set up in Belle's bedroom within the castle, which Meyer describes as "rich and lush, but cold and stark at the same time. It juxtaposes every little girl's fantasy of a fairy-tale bedroom with the reality that Belle is the Beast's prisoner and doesn't want to be there at all."

Meyer never considers a set as complete on its own; it needs the actors, the music, the lighting, the dancing, the staging. He treasures, for example, the moment when Belle goes up into the library: "I love the way her pink dress and the lighting combine with the set to create a small space of warmth and love within the cold, callous environment of the castle. It's a key visual moment."

Creating the Costumes

Collaboration is integral to Ann Hould-Ward's work as a costume designer. "Design," she insists, "is about fulfilling the needs of others; it is about being thoughtful and creative *with* other people, not just *on* them. With any design, you need to think about how people will use it and then, after building a prototype, watch them use it."

Hould-Ward began the design process by doing a tremendous amount of research. "You need to determine the period of a show and then research that

For Belle's bed, as well as other props and sets, the scenic design team translated Meyer's initial sketches into a detailed blueprint and then made a small three-dimensional model, using cardboard and glue. After the texture had been built up with gesso and modeling paste, Meyer painted the model as a guide for the scenic artists, who actually painted the finished, full-scale piece.

period from an artistic point of view," she explains. For *Beauty and the Beast*, she looked at teapots, clocks, and other objects from the mid- to later 1700s (the period of Beaumont's fairy tale) and studied paintings by such French rococo artists as Watteau, Fragonard, and Boucher. She also spent time familiarizing herself with the animated feature, which she wanted to honor in her designs, much as she had honored Georges Seurat's famous painting in her work on *Sunday in the Park with George.*

Although the research sparks ideas, Hould-Ward emphasizes that her designs must support the actors in telling their story to the audience. "The role is not the costume; the role is the actor," she stresses. With that in mind, she looked at each actor to determine what was best for that particular individual. The final creation of every costume came from carefully watching the performer on stage. "The real essence of the Beast's costume," she indicates, "comes from what I gleaned from Terrence Mann—what I could see in his movement and what he needed."

Designing the Enchanted Objects presented a special challenge because she had to make sure the actors could move well and the costumes didn't hamper their performance. Yet she also wanted the object that each costume represented to be immediately recognizable to the audience. "If you lined all the characters up, a four-year-old should be able to tell you who the people are," Hould-Ward says. "At the same time the costuming should be witty and intelligent enough to entertain the parents all evening."

Hould-Ward spent hours figuring out how, visually, a person might turn

In the animated feature (left) Gaston always wears his red jerkin. On stage, however, he shows us more of his wardrobe and puts on a yellow top (above). This new jerkin seems so much in character that if you didn't see the comparison, you might believe Gaston wore it in the movie.

152

into an object, how a collar might become the sconce of a candlestick or the front of a jacket become the face of a clock. "I wanted to lay out a plan for the actor to show how the transformation into an object was happening," she notes. With each costume, she maintained a "through" line—enlarging Mrs. Potts's cap until it became the top of a teapot or stiffening Cogsworth's epaulets into the ornate edging on a clock. At the end, when the servants are human again, there's no doubt about who's who, for their everyday clothes are in line with their object-like attire.

In addition to delighting audiences with their wit, the costumes offer a visual feast. Hould-Ward, who won a Tony award for her designs for *Beauty and the Beast,* is known for painting into her designs—actually brushing shadows into the creases of a jacket, for example—to give the costumes added dimension. "The texture of the costumes, the collaging together of different fabrics, the beading, and the painting all intensify the way you look at the person on stage," she explains. "It helps keep the focus on the actor. And it's also a fantastical place to take the eye."

Completing the Characters' Look

Working with Hould-Ward's designs, John Dods (who did fabricated effects for such films as *Ghostbusters II* and *Poltergeist III*) and David H. Lawrence (the hair designer for *Guys and Dolls, The Who's Tommy,* and many other Broadway shows) enhanced the impact of the Beast, the Enchanted Objects, and other characters. It was complicated work because all the elaborate headgear had to be light enough for the actors to wear it for a couple of hours. "Above all," stresses Lawrence, "we had to keep the actors' comfort in mind." Even an extra ounce of weight could make a headpiece unbearably heavy.

During rehearsals major changes were made in the Enchanted Objects' headpieces and the Beast's makeup to let the actors' performances come through. Lumiere, for example, had a wax drip for a nose, restricting his facial movements. "We were being upstaged by our costumes," actor Gary Beach recalls.

But that didn't last long. The night after the final dress rehearsal Dods received a directive to cut back the headpieces drastically to reveal much more of the actors' faces to the audience. "We practically remade the show from the neck up in a single day," he recollects. The Enchanted Objects, for example, had at first worn intricate headpieces in Act One that became even more elaborate in Act Two. Now it was decided to begin with more human hairstyles, introduce the Act One headpieces in Act Two, and dispense with the extreme forms altogether. Immediately, just in time for opening night, the actors' performances came alive.

To create the headpieces, as well as the Beast's visage, Dods used prosthetics, which he defines as "foam rubber or polyurethane pieces that are fitted in a precise way to the actors who wear them." He made a mold of the actor's head and then, using clay, sculpted prototypes of the pieces onto a plaster form of the actor's head, allowing everyone to see what the pieces would look like. Dods then made molds for these pieces. On later productions, with different actors, he cast

It takes three people over an hour to transform actor Terrence Mann step by step into the Beast. New rubber pieces are used for each performance.

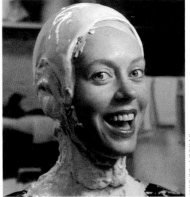

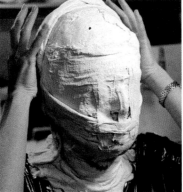

Actress Stacey Logan (top and center) has an alginate mold made of her head. Then a plaster form is made, and clay pieces are sculpted onto it to show Babette's ornate headpiece (bottom).

The plate steps on the "Be Our Guest" set are carefully spaced to let the dancers descend gracefully. The detailing of the large plate design is repeated in the dancers' costumes.

pieces from the original molds and adjusted them through a series of fittings.

Lawrence used Dods's plaster cast of Terrence Mann's head to create the Beast's mane of hair, but he also made his own models of each actor's head, drawing the hairline on a plastic bag and building up a ready-made mannequin form with tape to get the right head shape. For each of the more than 140 wigs in the show, he did research into eighteenth-century French hairstyles. Collaborating closely with Hould-Ward and Dods, he combined hints of the Enchantress's spell with hairdos from that period to suggest, for example, how Cogsworth's tightly curled coif might turn into a helmet or Lumiere's fluffy white pompadour might become a candle. The audience can almost see the change happening, magically, before their eyes.

Dancing Across the Stage

The choreography was intimately tied to the costuming. To envision the dancing in a show-stopping number like "Be Our Guest," choreographer Matt West first needed to know what kinds of objects would be dancing. With Hould-Ward he combed through kitchen supply stores, amassing a collection of corkscrews, egg timers, graters, and the like. As West relates, "We would hold up an object and ask, for example, 'If I were a spatula what would I look like and how would I move?' It took months to determine which objects worked best and whether they should be primarily singers or dancers."

Listening to the music for "Be Our Guest," which composer Menken describes as "Maurice Chevalier meets Busby Berkeley," West pictured plates walking down steps, Ziegfeld Follies style, as well as dancing flatware (referred to in the lyrics). It was only when he rehearsed the dancers in costume, however, that he could figure out exactly which movements would work best on stage. "I had to simplify a lot," he admits, "to make it look clean."

In choreographing, West works closely with assistant choreographer Dan Mojica and dance arranger Glen Kelly. Each dance number has its own "bible," a binder full of diagrams showing what each character does on each count of eight. "Even for the opening song in the town, which doesn't look highly choreographed, everybody walks or stops on a certain count," says West. A numbering system on the stage floor cues the dancers to where they should be. As West knows from his days dancing in *A Chorus Line,* if someone is not in exactly the right spot, the lighting may be off.

The Enchantment of Lighting

About 600 lights are used to bring out the magic of the fairy tale. (The lighting includes 55 Vari-lites, computerized moving lights—about four times as many as on any previous Broadway show.) "We chose a lot of saturated colors—deep blues and reds—for the lighting to give the scenes a quality *beyond* realism, a fairy-tale quality," says lighting designer Natasha Katz, who has lit such Broadway shows as *Gypsy* and *Someone Who'll Watch Over Me.*

Katz started out by asking the director about his intent: Should the show feel like the movie? Who was the audience? How would the characters and their costumes look? "All this information is the underpinning of lighting," she points out. "Lighting isn't just turning the lights on; it's trying to capture the whole environment and feel of the show."

Music adds another dimension to the lighting. "Every song creates a mood," explains Katz, "and the lighting can either go along with that mood or counterpoint it. The Beast's song, for example, is such a soul-searching number. At first the lighting isolates him within the castle, but then it shifts when the West Wing turns and you see him alone on the balcony. Initially we tried about 20 shafts of bright light on him, but that made him too powerful, too much like a superstar, which wasn't the intent of the piece. Instead, we wanted a more intro-spective feeling."

Deciding on the lighting required a lot of coordination with the costume and scenic designers. Katz wanted to be sure the audience could see the perform-ers' faces, that the actors wouldn't disappear into the sets. But most of all she wanted to help tell the story. "I hope people take away a feeling of magical joy, of a fairy tale come true," she says.

A Touch of Magic

The show's opening words, "Once upon a time," set the stage for magic, and with-in minutes a frightful hag metamorphoses into a glittering Enchantress, who throws a fiery ball to—poof!—cast her spell. "The fantastic and the out-of-the-ordinary are inherent to the story," points out director Roth. "The Enchantress, Chip, the magic rose, and the transformation of the Beast at the end were ideal for stage illusions. But all the magic had to be a part of the story. I didn't want the illusions to be there simply for their own sake—they had to help tell the story."

To create the illusions, Jim Steinmeyer and John Gaughan used magic principles over 100 years old, as well as new techniques that may surprise some professional magicians. "But the work on *Beauty and the Beast* was very different from a magic show," stresses Steinmeyer. "In a magic show the emphasis is on a trick that fools the audience; everything is subservient to that trick—it is the be-all and end-all of the show. In contrast, in *Beauty and the Beast* we had to be careful. While we wanted to achieve amazing effects, we didn't want to stop the show. The illusions had to flow integrally into the story, not stand out and feel different."

For Chip, Steinmeyer used four different illusions in various settings to enhance the boy-teacup's believability. "The tea cart, the tray that Mrs. Potts holds, the 'Be Our Guest' table, and the soup table are all aspects of the way you see Chip," he explains. "By giving you different views, which you reassemble in your mind, you end up with a fuller picture."

Steinmeyer adds, "I love the moment at the end, when the boy Chip runs out into his mother's arms, and people applaud. It shows that the illusion worked, that people on some level believed this boy had been turned into a teacup, and only now that the spell is broken, is he a person again."

BRIAN PRESS

Only when the spell is broken does Chip run on stage, freely using his arms and legs. For most of the show, all of the actor's body below his neck is hidden. His acting is limited to subtle head motions and facial and vocal expressions; moreover, he must constantly take care not to move the rest of his body too much—or he will destroy the illusion.

Made of fire-retardant polyurethane foam and sprayed with five layers of high-heat-resistant paint, Lumiere's hands rise about four inches above the sconce. Each flame uses about an ounce of liquid butane fuel per show.

Although he won't reveal the secret of the Beast's transformation, Steinmeyer underlines, "The illusion really benefits from the emotion in the story leading up to that moment. It's as if we got to put the cherry on top of an ice cream sundae; everything you've seen on stage has been building toward this point."

In fact, Steinmeyer says, all the elements of the production are a bit magical—from the story to the lighting and the costumes. "The audience watching the show is there to see a fairy tale brought to life," he points out. "It's a purely magical world, and the illusions naturally form a part of that world."

Some of the most spectacular magic involves pyrotechnic devices designed by Tylor Wymer of Walt Disney Theatrical Productions. Two pieces created especially for the show—the Enchantress's fireball and Lumiere's flaming hands —are so novel they hold U.S. patents.

"It was very difficult to design a fireball that the Enchantress ignites and actually throws," Wymer indicates. "We wanted it to be totally safe, very precise, and controlled." For protection, the Enchantress wears a special fireproofed glove extending from her elbow to her fingertips; she also undergoes intense training to feel comfortable holding on to the burning ball for a moment before throwing it.

Lumiere's hands had to be safe, easy to maintain, and light enough for the actor to wear for over two hours. Actor Beach was given warm-up and cool-

The steam that emerges from Mrs. Potts's arm is actually smoke created by a special pyrotechnic device. The smoke is scented, so if someone gets a whiff, it doesn't smell bad.

down exercises, but he wasn't prepared for the other actors' reactions: "Eleanor Glockner [Madame de la Grande Bouche] asked me, 'Did you notice at first you were usually standing alone backstage?' No one knew how the flames worked, so they stood about five feet away."

Excitement Backstage

As the audience watches the fairy tale unfold on stage, another drama, full of suspense, is going on backstage. At any one time 30 to 35 actors may be changing costumes while almost 70 crew members help dress the actors, prepare the sets,

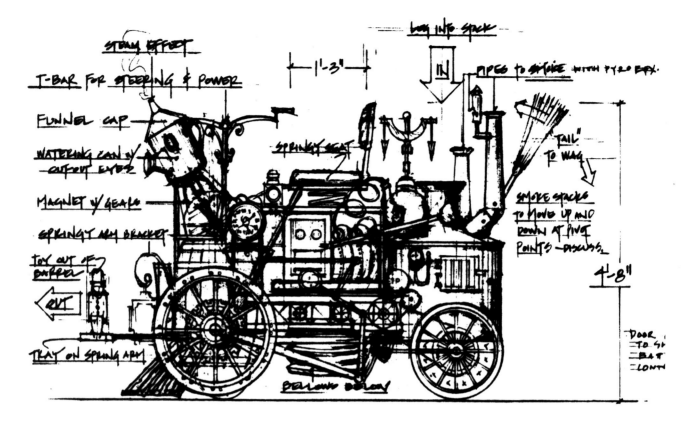

The labels on the blueprint read:
STEAM EFFECT
T-BAR FOR STEERING & POWER
FUNNEL CAP
WATERING CAN W/ CUTOUT EYES
MAGNET W/ GEARS
SPRINGY ARM BRACKET
TOY OUT OF BARREL
OUT
TRAY ON SPRING ARM
1'-3"
LOG INTO STACK
IN
PIPES TO STAGE WITH PYRO EFX.
SPRINGY SEAT
"TAIL" TO WAG
SMOKE STACKS TO MOVE UP AND DOWN AT FIVE POINTS — DISCUSS.
4'-8"
DOOR TO SL BAT LOFT
BELLOWS BELOW

The hodgepodge look of Maurice's invention is carefully planned, as this blueprint shows. The contraption includes a wireless device that is basically a modified security alarm system. As a result, a technician backstage can trigger the machine's performance—making it sputter, explode, or chop wood—while Maurice sits on top.

check the technical elements, make instant repairs, and operate the computers. "I wish we could give people a glimpse of all the activity backstage," says director Roth, "because it's an incredible ballet, very tightly choreographed, so that everything gets done quickly and efficiently."

"There's as much of a human element behind the scenes as in front of the audience," adds production supervisor Jeremiah Harris. "*People* are responsible for what happens on stage—for every time the scenery flies in, a drop moves, smoke pours in, or the lights flash, for example."

State-of-the-art computers help coordinate the many elements, from scenery to lighting to sound. "Computers allow us to do what was previously unimaginable," notes Harris. The heavy castle set, for example, can be moved instantly and precisely along its track. Or Maurice's invention can spark and explode, seemingly on its own.

But humans are still involved in the process. When Gaston punches Lefou, someone hits a bar on a computer to produce the sound of the blow. The timing must be right every single time.

The complexity of the sound system is amazing, with 20 wireless channels of communication and 34 microphone systems for the cast. Hundreds of sound effects occur throughout the show, including the Beast's roars. "To get a frightening noise, we combined the sound of an animal's cry with Terrence Mann's live roar," explains sound designer T. Richard Fitzgerald, "but it all sounds as if it came from the Beast."

Giving the Characters Life

The enthusiasm of the actors brings the show to life each night on the stage. "We looked for actors who would honor the animation but also had strong personalities of their own to make the characters three-dimensional," says casting director Jay Binder. "Credibility is essential: You have to believe it's Gaston, for example, before he even opens his mouth."

Director Robert Jess Roth agrees. "We discussed each character's function in the story: how Mrs. Potts is the Beast's surrogate mother, for example, or Lumiere is the Beast's dashing romantic coach. Then we looked for people who embodied the spirit of these characters."

During the rehearsals the actors added their interpretations to the characters, sometimes improving on their lines. "At a certain point they knew their characters better than I did," scriptwriter Linda Woolverton remarks, "because each actor was living just his or her character all the way through, from the beginning to the end of the story, every night."

For the actors every performance is a new challenge. Each time, as Susan Egan (Belle) has explained to one journalist, "you've got to prove it all over again. And you keep growing. Each show is really better than the last one."

A harmonious working relationship between the actors underlies the show's success. "There's a really good feeling backstage before the show," notes Roth. "Everyone wants to be there, and that enthusiasm translates into the energy and warmth that comes through to the audience."

"If we look like we're having a great time and care about each other—it's true," underlines Beth Fowler (Mrs. Potts). "You can't tell a wonderful warm story like *Beauty and the Beast* unless you already have that warmth inside you."

Thanks to the Audience

For everyone both on stage and behind the scenes, it is the response of the audience that matters most. "The audience feeds the performance," emphasizes Gary Beach (Lumiere). "To hear the children laughing, the fathers and mothers laughing—all enjoying this event together—refreshes and rewards us."

Terrence Mann (the Beast) agrees. "The audiences are terrific," he exclaimed on television. As he told one reporter, "It's a wonderful story that has simple truths that reach everybody."

"We wanted to appeal to people of all ages," producer Robert McTyre points out, "and it's especially exciting to see thousands of children coming to the show. We hope we can rebuild the tradition of children going to live theater, because that's how many of us working on the show got started—by going to the theater when we were children."

Disney's Beauty and the Beast opens the door on the magical world of live theater to everyone, from age two to ninety. Michael Eisner, Disney's chairman, hopes "that the show will be a lifelong memory for a new generation of theatergoers, and that it will bring a new meaning to the word *Disney* for veteran theatergoers."

Index

TYPOGRAPHY
The type in this book is set in Centaur MT, regular and italic,
with liberal use of swash characters in the headings.
Old style figures and ligatures were used throughout.

PRINTING AND BINDING
Film prepared by Oceanic Graphic Printing, Hong Kong
Printed and bound by RR Donnelley, Willard, Ohio
Jacket printed by Phoenix Color, Lanham, Maryland

1

2

4

7

4

6

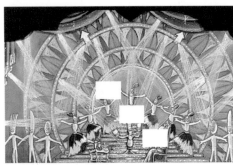

8

9